"Marry you? I don't know you," Jenna insisted vehemently.

He almost smiled at her tone, but the subject was too serious. Taking her hand in his, he let his thumb skim the top of it. He could feel her slight quiver and experienced his own start of desire. There was chemistry between them as well as a child.

"Would marriage be so terrible?" he asked in a voice he didn't recognize because it was filled with tenderness and protectiveness he'd never felt for a woman in his adult life. "I'm proposing a partnership. We'd live together, eventually sleep together."

"Sleep together?"

The look in her eyes was part fear, part panic, with a spark of interest. If he trod very carefully, he might get what he wanted.

Turning her hand over, he brought it to his lips and kissed her palm, never taking his eyes from her. "There's attraction between us, Jenna, whether you want to admit it or not."

Dear Reader,

Your best bet for coping with April showers is to run—not walk—to your favorite retail outlet and check out this month's lineup. We'd like to highlight popular author Laurie Paige and her new miniseries SEVEN DEVILS. Laurie writes, "On my way to a writers' conference in Denver, I spotted the Seven Devils Mountains. This had to be checked out! Sure enough, the rugged, fascinating land proved to be ideal for a bunch of orphans who'd been demanding that their stories be told." You won't want to miss *Showdown!*, the second book in the series, which is about a barmaid and a sheriff destined for love!

Gina Wilkins dazzles us with *Conflict of Interest,* the second book in THE McCLOUDS OF MISSISSIPPI series, which deals with the combustible chemistry between a beautiful literary agent and her ruggedly handsome and reclusive author. Can they have some fun without love taking over the relationship? Don't miss Marilyn Pappano's *The Trouble with Josh,* which features a breast cancer survivor who decides to take life by storm and make the most of everything—but she never counts on sexy cowboy Josh Rawlins coming into the mix.

In Peggy Webb's *The Mona Lucy,* a meddling but well-meaning mother attempts to play Cupid to her son and a beautiful artist who is painting her portrait. Karen Rose Smith brings us *Expecting the CEO's Baby,* an adorable tale about a mix-up at the fertility clinic and a marriage of convenience between two strangers. And in Lisette Belisle's *His Pretend Wife,* an accident throws an ex-con and an ex-debutante together, making them discover that rather than enemies, they just might be soul mates!

As you can see, we have a variety of stories for our readers, which explore the essentials—life, love and family. Stay tuned next month for six more top picks from Special Edition!

Sincerely,

Karen Taylor Richman
Senior Editor

Please address questions and book requests to:
Silhouette Reader Service
U.S.: 3010 Walden Ave., P.O. Box 1325, Buffalo, NY 14269
Canadian: P.O. Box 609, Fort Erie, Ont. L2A 5X3

Expecting the CEO's Baby

KAREN ROSE SMITH

SPECIAL EDITION™

Published by Silhouette Books

America's Publisher of Contemporary Romance

To my son, Ken. Dreams are a reach away.
May light and love always surround you in the reaching.

To Suzanne. May each of your days
be filled with the wonder in Sydney's eyes.

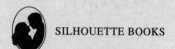 SILHOUETTE BOOKS

ISBN 0-373-24535-1

EXPECTING THE CEO'S BABY

Copyright © 2003 by Karen Rose Smith

Visit Silhouette at www.eHarlequin.com

Printed in U.S.A.

KAREN ROSE SMITH,

a former teacher and home decorator, has been a mother for thirty years. She believes motherhood is the most rewarding, life-altering experience a woman can have. Blessed with a husband who helped in all aspects of parenting, she drew on those memories for Jenna's and Blake's development in this book. Readers can write to her c/o Silhouette Books or e-mail through her Web site at Karen@karenrosesmith.com.

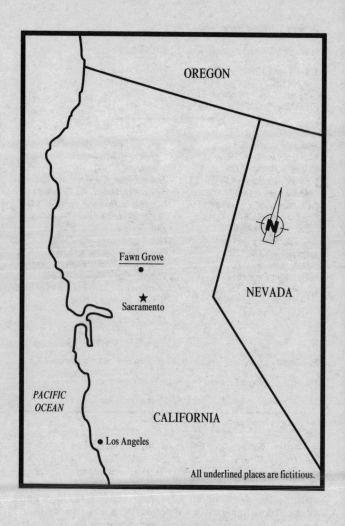

OREGON

NEVADA

Fawn Grove

★
Sacramento

PACIFIC
OCEAN

CALIFORNIA

● Los Angeles

All underlined places are fictitious.

Chapter One

Everyone was staring at her!

As the receptionist showed Jenna Winton into the large conference room, a frisson of foreboding skipped up her spine, and she protectively laid her hand over her rounding belly. She'd been awakened this Monday morning by a few kicks from the child who was already the center of her world. More was right with her world now than it had been in the year and a half since B.J. had died. Still...

Before she'd even dressed, she'd received a phone call from the Emerson Fertility Clinic, the clinic that had implanted her with her deceased husband's sperm. She'd been summoned here to a meeting this afternoon, and the receptionist wouldn't tell her what it was about.

Now as Jenna looked at the faces around the table, recognizing her doctor, his nurse and two more men she didn't know, her heart pounded and she told herself to stay calm. There was no reason for alarm. Maybe they just wanted to discuss her payment plan. She was behind a month.

Her physician, Dr. Palmer, gave her a smile that was perfunctory at best. With silver hair and in his fifties, he'd always welcomed her with a smile and a paternal attitude that had made her feel comfortable. She expected him to state the reason the clinic had called her, but instead, one of the men she didn't recognize smiled a plastic smile.

"Good morning, Mrs. Winton." He extended his hand to her. "I'm Tom Franklin, the director of Emerson Fertility Clinic. Beside me is Wayne Schlessinger, the clinic's counsel. I think you know everyone else."

"Yes, I do." Jenna was becoming more concerned by the minute. The atmosphere in the small room was charged, and she didn't understand any of it.

"Please have a seat," Mr. Franklin invited, motioning to a chair beside his at the head of the table.

Everyone was still watching her. As the director's gaze passed over her shoulder-length, light-brown hair, her white knit T-shirt under the pink maternity jumper, she sensed he was sizing her up and she didn't like the feeling.

Gripping her straw purse, Jenna slipped into the chair gratefully, uneasy with being the center of attention.

Mr. Franklin hardly gave her time to take a breath before he began, "You're probably wondering why we called you here today."

"If it's my late payment, I'll be sending it to you within the week."

"No, no, nothing like that. And let me assure you

there is nothing wrong with your pregnancy, either. According to your chart, everything is just as it should be in your sixth month.''

''Then I don't understand.''

He rubbed his hand across his forehead. ''There's no easy way to say this, Mrs. Winton. A mistake was made the day you were inseminated. Instead of being inseminated with your husband's sperm, you were inseminated with another man's sperm, Blake Winston's. When the technician checked the names on the canisters, she removed B. *Winston's* canister rather than B. *Winton's* canister. Both men are from Fawn Grove, and with the likeness in the names, she selected the wrong one.''

Her heart racing, Jenna knew she must have misunderstood Thomas Franklin. ''I *can't* be carrying someone else's child! You froze B.J.'s sperm before he started chemo because we thought he'd get better and we wanted to have children.''

Franklin's hand covered hers. ''I know, Mrs. Winton. I also know after your husband died, you came to us and Dr. Palmer decided to go forward with you to help you conceive your husband's child. Unfortunately, the technician was overwrought the day you were inseminated. Her own husband was critically ill and her mind was on getting back to the hospital to see him. I'm sure you can understand that.''

Jenna understood all too well.

''This type of thing has never happened here before and we *will* take precautions to make sure it never happens again. We've terminated the technician.''

Everything he'd said was beginning to sink in, and Jenna felt overwhelmed with the enormity of it. ''Why didn't your technician admit her mistake sooner?''

As Franklin looked to the clinic's lawyer, Wayne Schlessinger explained, "The day after the procedure she realized what had happened because she noticed the wrong vial was marked that sperm had been removed. But she has two children, and hers was the only salary. With her husband in the hospital, their bills had mounted up. She was afraid, and rightly so, that she'd lose her position here if she confessed."

"Why did she confess now?" Jenna almost wished she hadn't, then she could have gone on, blissfully ignorant of this terrible mistake.

"Her husband is back at work now, and the burden of carrying this knowledge was too great. She couldn't keep her secret any longer. She wanted to tell you all this in person, but we thought it was better if she didn't appear here today."

Jenna didn't know if Mr. Franklin was right or wrong about that. Maybe it would have been easier if she could have put a human face to this mistake. The more she thought about all the details surrounding it, the less she had to face the fact that the baby she was carrying *wasn't* B.J.'s.

Schlessinger added, "The clinic will take full responsibility for its employee's error. We asked you here today to forestall legal action. We don't feel that would be beneficial to either of us. If you will sign the proper documents, in exchange, we will give you a settlement of one hundred thousand dollars. We have that check here for you today."

Sliding a legal-looking form before her, he held out a pen, obviously fully expecting her to sign it.

Anger and frustration at Emerson Fertility Clinic rushed through Blake early Monday evening as he climbed the outside steps to Jenna Winton's second-floor apartment. The early June late-day sun shone brightly, but Blake hardly noticed it or the crumbling stucco in the stairwell of the apartment complex located in an older section of Fawn Grove. His thoughts swirled around the meeting he'd just had at the Sacramento clinic and the revelation that there was a woman in Fawn Grove carrying his child. Franklin hadn't wanted to give him Jenna Winton's address, but the board at the clinic knew the kind of influence he could wield.

Reaching the second floor, Blake found apartment 112-C and pressed the doorbell, not exactly sure what he was going to say. He was about to press the bell a second time when the door opened.

He'd been given the details, and he knew Jenna Winton was six months pregnant. Yet when he was suddenly confronted with her pretty but obviously worried face, her wavy light brown hair caught in a gold barrette above her right temple, her dark brown eyes filled with questions because a strange man was at her door, he lost his grip on the confidence and power that usually got him what he wanted when he wanted it.

As her gaze passed over his hand-tailored charcoal suit, his black hair, the lines and creases that thirty-seven years had etched onto his face, she asked, "Can I help you?"

Her rounding belly was lost in the folds of her pink jumper. Blake had a visceral reaction to the idea that this woman was carrying his child. Frozen emotions began to thaw and a corner of his heart opened. Jenna Winton, who looked wholesome, innocent and vulnerable, shook the foundation of his world.

"Do you always open your door so readily to strangers?'' Fawn Grove, located about a half hour from Sacramento, was growing quickly. Its small-town innocence wouldn't last forever.

Without becoming defensive, Jenna gave him a tremulous smile. ''This is Fawn Grove, not Sacramento or L.A. Are you checking security in the building?''

Ironic that she should think that. After all, security systems and strategies had made him the success he was. ''I wish it were something that simple,'' he told her, struck again by her delicate beauty, her pregnant radiance that he'd never seen on a woman before. ''I'm Blake Winston.''

At that, Jenna Winton's face paled and her troubled brown gaze studied him. ''I'm not sure we should talk. I just got off the phone with my lawyer and—''

''Mrs. Winton, we *have* to talk. I'm the father of that child you're carrying. You can't expect me to leave here without discussing this.''

After a few moments of hesitation, she stepped back inside the apartment to let him pass. He caught the scent of a light, flowery perfume—lilacs—as he stepped into her living room and realized it was as hot as blazes in there. He ridged his starched shirt collar with his finger.

Noticing, Jenna apologized. ''I'm sorry it's so hot in here. The air-conditioning broke down last night. The landlord is attending to it.'' She'd opened two windows that looked out onto the back courtyard, but not a wisp of a breeze stirred.

They stared at each other for long, silent moments, and Blake could feel a different kind of heat in the air. She was looking at him with those big brown eyes.... The stirring of desire had to be in his imagination. He wasn't attracted to women like Jenna Winton. He went for leggy blondes who knew the score.

Suddenly his gaze dropped to Jenna's hands. She was twisting the gold band on her left ring finger—her wedding band.

"Why did you come?" she asked, looking fearful but a bit defiant all at the same time.

He'd come to get a look at her, to see if she'd be a suitable surrogate. He hadn't intended to hire one for a few more years, but faced with the reality of what had happened, he had no choice but to look at the situation realistically now.

"Why don't we sit down," he suggested, taking charge, hoping to put both of them a little more at ease.

She looked grateful he'd made the suggestion. As she sat in an old wooden rocker with carvings on the back, he took the opportunity to glance around at the brightly flowered chintz sofa covering, the lace curtains at the windows, the bookshelves and the desk where she probably prepared her lessons. He'd learned from a swift computer background check that she was a second-grade teacher.

Settling himself on the sofa across from her, he tried to be casual about the situation that was anything *but* casual. "I just came from a meeting at the clinic."

She swallowed hard. "I guess it was quite a shock for you, too. I'm still having a difficult time believing this. B.J. and I wanted a child desperately."

"B.J.?"

"My husband. His name was Barry Jacob but everyone called him B.J."

"I understand he died a year and a half ago." Blake knew he didn't have the capacity in his heart for much compassion anymore. He'd hardened himself to the cruelties of life. Yet with Jenna Winton, he found a corner of it aching for her.

Meeting his gaze courageously, she nodded. "He had cancer and we had his sperm frozen before treatments started, fully expecting he'd recover. We always wanted a family...." She cleared her throat, trying to stave off emotion. "But B.J. didn't recover. After he was gone, I decided having his child would always keep him alive in my heart."

What would it be like, Blake wondered, to have a woman love him with that much fervor and faithfulness? He'd learned as a teenager a woman's loyalty only extended as far as her selfish interests. He was hoping that would be the case with Jenna Winton, also. Sentiment didn't pay the bills. According to the databases he'd accessed, she was deeply in debt for the hospital expenses her insurance hadn't covered when her husband was ill, as well as for the insemination procedure. "The clinic told me you didn't accept the settlement they offered."

"I know better than to sign anything without consulting a lawyer. Fortunately I have a friend whose husband practices law. Did you accept the settlement?" she asked, surprising him.

"A settlement isn't what I'm after." As he studied Jenna Winton now, he knew instinctively she'd be the perfect surrogate. All he had to do was convince her of that. "I want the child you're carrying."

She looked stunned by his announcement and appeared to be speechless.

"I suppose you're right to hold out for a bigger settlement from the clinic," he continued. "They owe you big-time. But if you act as my surrogate..."

He took a check from his inside suit-coat pocket and offered it to her.

Her eyes widened as she noted the figure.

"That should cover your medical and hospital expenses, time off work and a little extra for going through the whole ordeal. If the amount is suitable, we can sign the papers and at delivery, you'll give the baby to me."

As they'd talked, heat had been building in the small living room along with the tension. Jenna's brow was damp and she swiped her hand across it now as she stared at the check he was holding.

Then in a matter of moments, she went from speechless astonishment to fiery indignation. It flared in her beautiful brown eyes as she jumped to her feet, glaring at Blake as if he were crazy. "I don't know who you think you are, Mr. Winston, but I want no part of your money. This baby is mine, and I'm not giving her or him up to anyone."

Pretty before, she was beautiful now, and Blake felt a startling bolt of desire shoot through him that he couldn't deny. Ignoring it, he stood, too, and faced her. "Why would you want to keep a child by a man you don't even know?"

The question didn't throw her as he'd expected it to. "I might not know *you,* Mr. Winston, but I know this child. I've been carrying him for six months. I love this baby. I've sung to him, felt him moving inside me. I will never give him up."

Blake's shirt stuck to his back, and he could feel sweat beading on his brow. "You might not have any choice."

His warning rattled Jenna. He could see the fear in

her eyes as all the implications of their situation became clear.

Hurrying to the door, she opened it. "I think you'd better leave."

No one dismissed Blake. After Preston Howard—the father of the girl Blake had imagined himself in love with—had done that to him nineteen long years ago, Blake had vowed no one would ever dismiss him again. Standing his ground, he said evenly, "With the money I'm offering, together with the settlement from the clinic, you'd be set for a while."

Her spine straightened and her shoulders squared. "Obviously, Mr. Winston, you don't know me. If you did, you'd realize I'm more sentimental than I am practical. Bonds and family mean more to me than money ever could. So don't bother making your offer again because I won't accept it. Please leave or I'll call the apartment complex manager."

This time he did as she demanded because he could see her hands were shaking and her chin was quivering. She was pregnant with his child, and he didn't want anything to happen to the baby or to her. Yet he couldn't let her think she'd won, either, because she hadn't.

Before he crossed the threshold, he looked her squarely in the eyes. "You'll be hearing from my lawyer."

When Jenna closed the door behind Blake Winston, she almost collapsed against it. The emotions from everything that had happened today, along with the heat, seemed to press against her, making her short of breath. She knew she couldn't let her emotions affect her physically. She had this baby to protect, and she would do that with her dying breath.

Closing her eyes for a few moments, thinking of the ocean and sand and waves, she calmed herself and her breathing became more even. Spinning around, she peered out the peephole. Blake Winston had indeed left. Not wasting a moment, she crossed to the cordless phone, picked it up and went to the window to catch a breeze. She pressed redial and hoped Rafe Pierson hadn't left his law office. She hoped he wasn't with a client. She hoped he could allay her fears. When she reached his receptionist, she gave her name again and the woman put her through.

Jenna had met Rafe's wife, Shannon, through the elementary school where she taught. Shannon was a psychologist who used equine-assisted therapy to help troubled children. Three years ago, Jenna had heard about her success rate and recommended her services to the parents of one of her students. Shannon had invited Jenna to the Rocky R to give her a glimpse into her methods. She'd stayed for supper and gotten to know Shannon as well as her husband, Rafe, and their two girls. Grateful for the friendship that had begun before B.J. had died, Jenna couldn't imagine discussing all of this with a complete stranger. Her upbringing as a minister's daughter had taught her to keep her own counsel, to watch whatever she said and did because it would reflect favorably or unfavorably on her father. She'd never wavered from that course until she'd decided to be artificially inseminated with B.J.'s sperm. Her father had disapproved, but this time his disapproval hadn't mattered.

"Jenna?" Rafe asked, his voice carrying honest concern. "What's wrong? Has the clinic contacted you again?"

"No. Blake Winston has. He made me an offer he

thought I couldn't refuse to become a surrogate for him.''

Rafe swore. That was the first time Jenna had ever heard him use a vulgarity. As a former D.A., he usually kept his temper well in check. ''What did you tell him?''

''I told him the child is mine. It is, isn't it, Rafe? He said his lawyer would be in touch. He can't really take this baby away from me, can he?''

There was a long moment of silence. ''This is an area of the law that's changing day by day. I can't tell you Winston doesn't have a leg to stand on because in reality, he *is* the biological father. If this was anyone but Blake Winston…''

''I don't understand. Do you know him?'' Rafe hadn't mentioned knowing him in their last conversation.

''No, I don't know him. I know *of* him. He has plenty of money and just as much influence. He grew up in Fawn Grove, then made a fortune in L.A. in security systems. He's the CEO of a company that not only installs security but arranges it for politicians and stars.''

''And he lives in Fawn Grove?''

''He returned about three years ago and set up a branch of his company in Sacramento. He bought the Van Heusen mansion.''

Truth be told, Jenna didn't read the paper often. As a teacher, her nights were spent correcting papers or doing lesson plans. Nevertheless, she knew the Van Heusen house and grounds. It was located at the northern end of town. As a child, she and her brother Gary had taken walks past it, wondering what it would be like to live in a house like that.

"And you believe his money will make a difference?" she asked, more than worried now.

"It's not his money, Jenna. I'm just as concerned about his influence. Hold on a minute. Donna is passing me a message that came in on the other line."

Jenna wondered how a judge would look at Blake Winston's money and his mansion, as well as what he could offer a child.

"Jenna?"

"Yes, I'm still here."

"The clinic called and they want a meeting."

She'd given the clinic Rafe's name and number, knowing she was going to let him handle this for her. "What kind of meeting?"

"They didn't say, but I'll find out. Are you free tomorrow?"

School was closed for summer vacation and her only commitment was filling in for her father's secretary when Shirley left on vacation at the end of the week. But she'd fit in this meeting anytime. "Yes, I'm free."

"Good. I suspect Winston and his lawyer will be there, too. In the meantime I'll research case law on this. We'll go in there as prepared as we possibly can be."

"Rafe, I know I should give you a retainer or something—"

"Right now I'm your lawyer because I'm your friend. If it gets drawn out, we'll talk about retainers. Okay?"

"I really don't know how to thank you."

"I'll tell you how you can thank me. This has been a rough day for you. Get yourself a lemonade, put your feet up and try to do something mindless until tomorrow. I'll get back to you with the time of the meeting."

After Jenna had thanked Rafe again and given him her cell phone number, she hung up knowing she couldn't stay here in the apartment in the heat. She'd stop at the ice cream parlor for a frozen lemonade and then go to the library. Maybe there in the air-conditioning, she could use their computers and do research concerning custody cases on her own. What bothered her the most about all of this was the quickening of her pulse and the roller coaster waves she'd felt when she'd looked into Blake Winston's eyes. B.J. had been the salt of the earth, the consummate common man. He'd been a roofer and never aspired to more than that, living each day as it came. Through their years together, he'd convinced Jenna to do the same. She'd loved him with all her heart.

But she'd never had the reaction to B.J. that she'd had to Blake Winston. This rich man, the father of her child, made her pulse race in a way that had nothing to do with her pregnancy. That troubled her, almost as much as Blake's warning that she'd hear from his lawyer.

As Rafe escorted Jenna on Tuesday afternoon into the same conference room where the bomb had been dropped on her yesterday, her gaze passed over her physician, Dr. Palmer, the clinic's director, Thomas Franklin, the clinic's counsel, Wayne Schlessinger, and a man she didn't know. Then her gaze locked to Blake Winston's. His smoky-gray eyes told her he was a complicated man. The fluttering of her stomach, which she'd like to attribute to anxiety and fear—but couldn't if she wanted to be honest with herself—told her something else entirely. Seated at the end of the conference table, he was wearing a light blue polo shirt, navy casual slacks and supple leather loafers. Just noticing all of this made her feel as if she were betraying B.J.'s memory. Yet noticing Blake Winston's clothes was a far better distraction than noticing the width of his shoulders, the beard line along his jaw, the vitality of his thick black hair.

"Mrs. Winton," Wayne Schlessinger said in greeting.

"Mr. Schlessinger," she acknowledged, and gave a little nod to everyone else, including her adversary.

After Schlessinger shook hands with Rafe, he motioned Jenna and her lawyer to two chairs on the opposite side of the table from the clinic's representatives. Jenna found herself seated beside Blake, and an uncomfortable situation became unbearable. She was too aware of his cologne, too aware of his appraising glance as his gaze passed over her white-and-blue smocked maternity dress.

Schlessinger addressed Rafe. "I take it you've carefully read our settlement offer?"

"Yes, I have. But I haven't advised Jenna to sign it."

"May I ask why not?"

"I want her to be sure that she's ready to waive her rights to any future lawsuits before she signs anything. It was unfair of you to pressure her to take the offer yesterday."

"There was no pressure, Mr. Pierson."

Jenna clasped Rafe's arm, telling him she wanted to speak for herself. "Having a $100,000 check ready for me to endorse was pressure in itself, Mr. Schlessinger." She looked at Blake. "Are *you* taking their offer?"

He repeated what he'd told her yesterday. "The clinic's money isn't the issue. My child is."

"Mr. Winston," Schlessinger interrupted. "We've gathered everyone here today to try to resolve this."

"Resolve this?" Rafe asked wryly. "My client entered into a contract with you in good faith. She's carried this child for six months. Do you think any amount of money is going to make up for the mistake your clinic made?" He directed his attention to Blake. "Do you think any amount of money will convince my client to give up her child?"

There was frustration on Blake's face as well as a blaze of anger in his eyes as he answered. "If money won't do it, then the law might. I'm the biological father of this child and I have rights. Joint custody at the very least. You're right about one thing, Mr. Pierson, this isn't going to be resolved today. Not unless your client is willing to sign a surrogate agreement and give up rights to the child when it's born."

Feeling as if she'd been struck by a lightning bolt, Jenna realized her child meant so much to this man that he'd use all of his power and influence to take away her baby. Although she'd been dealing with the situation since yesterday, she suddenly felt overwhelmed by it all. The information she'd read on the Internet hadn't been encouraging, and the idea that she was having a child that wasn't B.J.'s filled her with the same grief she'd experienced after he died. In the midst of the grief, she heard her father's voice warning her against being artificially inseminated because it wasn't natural.

Now she was going to have to tell her father she wasn't even carrying B.J.'s child! She was carrying a stranger's child, and this stranger wanted to take her child away from her—or at the very least, share custody with her.

Tears she'd been holding at bay for more than twenty-four hours sprang to the surface. There was no way she could hide them. Yet she wasn't going to make a fool of herself in front of all these people.

Pushing away from the table so fast her chair tipped over, she fled the conference room. She heard Rafe's voice but didn't stop, couldn't stop, wouldn't stop…not until she'd rushed through the waiting room, pushed open the door and fled around the corner of the building to the parking lot. There under the shade of a live oak, she let the tears freely fall while she covered her face with her hands, wishing against all odds that this was a nightmare and she'd soon awaken.

When she felt a hand on her shoulder, she took a breath, choked back a sob and looked up, expecting to see Rafe. But it wasn't Rafe who stood there. It was Blake Winston, the man who wanted her baby for his own, the man who'd replaced B.J. in her dreams last night.

She turned away from him, trying to hide her tears, trying to hide feelings she didn't understand.

Chapter Two

Blake hadn't chased after a woman since he was eighteen. That escapade had ended in disaster with a sense of betrayal that yawned so wide he hadn't been interested in a serious relationship since. Yet when Jenna Winton had run out of that conference room, he'd known *he* was the reason. What he'd seen on her face was genuine distress.

Now, for the first time since his meeting with the director of the clinic yesterday, he tried to put himself in her shoes. She'd loved her husband—so much so that she wanted to carry his child even when he was gone. The news that she wasn't carrying B.J. Winton's child must have been devastating. Another woman might have wanted nothing to do with the baby. That's fully what Blake had expected. Compensating Jenna Winton for her pregnancy and her services as a surrogate had seemed a reasonable and perfect solution to him.

Yet apparently she'd formed a bond with this child already and didn't want to let go. If she was that kind of woman, she would make a wonderful mother.

"Jenna," he murmured, using her given name as if it was his right. She was still turned away from him, and he realized she didn't want him to see her tears.

Women used tears to manipulate. They used tears to bring a man to his knees, didn't they?

Watching the sunlight play on the blond strands in Jenna's light brown hair, seeing the tension in her small shoulders as she tried to keep her turmoil from him, compassion he hadn't felt in a very long time stirred in his heart along with something else...something else he didn't want to identify or examine.

Clasping her shoulder, he nudged her around. Still she kept her head bent, and he couldn't keep from lifting her chin so she'd meet his gaze.

Her skin was soft, a creamy ivory under his tanned thumb. The few freckles on her nose attested to the fact that she wasn't wearing makeup. Her lips were a bit pinker than natural and he suspected she'd applied lipstick. Not that sticky, shiny concoction that made women's lips look like they were painted, but a creamy soft pink that suited her well. It was her dark brown eyes that made his chest tighten. They were swimming with tears and anguish, testifying to the fact that this wasn't a performance for his benefit.

"I'm sorry if I upset you," he said gently, realizing he meant it.

When she tried to blink away her tears, they rolled down her cheeks and she swiped at them self-consciously. "After B.J. died, I felt lost. Then I became pregnant and life seemed to have meaning again. Now you're threatening to take away my baby and—''

The urge to take this woman into his arms was so strong Blake had to fight it with every ounce of his self-control. She had to look up a good six inches to meet his gaze, and although she was pregnant, she still looked slender and fragile. Yet from the way she'd stood up to him already, he suspected she wasn't fragile at all.

''I do want this child, and I imagined I'd go about it just as I have everything else over the past twenty years,'' he found himself explaining. ''I've always set goals and reached for them, not letting anything alter my course.''

A tear she hadn't managed to wipe away stole down her cheek. Before he thought better of it, he caught it and let his finger glide over her skin. This time her eyes didn't waver from his, and he found himself aroused by simply touching her. The space around them seemed to be charged with a current that could shake the leaves from the trees.

''I can see now,'' he went on hoarsely, ''having a baby is quite different from opening a branch of my firm in another city, finding the best people to work with me, or topping last year's revenue.''

The hum of cars on the street in front of the clinic was a backdrop to the most important conversation of his life.

Jenna's gaze was troubled as she asked, ''How can we settle this if we both want the same thing and neither of us will let go? You just learned about this child yesterday. I've been nourishing this baby and talking to it and playing music for it for the past six months. This is *my* child, Mr. Winston.''

"Blake," he corrected her. "It's Blake," he said again. "Do you mind if I call you Jenna? Formality will only get in the way of whatever decisions we have to make."

"That's just it, Mr...." She stopped herself. "Blake. What decisions can we make if we both want to be parents?"

"I don't know. I do know I think you and I have to talk about this without our lawyers. We need to spend some time together and discuss what all of this means to our lives."

"I wouldn't advise that, Jenna," Rafe said from behind Blake's shoulder. "Mr. Winston has had a lot more practice than you persuading other people to do his bidding."

Stepping back, Jenna made space to include Rafe in the discussion. "I can listen to him, Rafe. Mr...." she stopped herself once more. "Blake isn't going to convince me to do anything I shouldn't."

Then she gave her lawyer a weak smile. "I have to persuade twenty-five children every day to do exactly what they're supposed to do. My persuasive skills might be on par with Mr. Winston's." She looked up at him almost apologetically for forgetting to use his first name again.

No matter how upset Jenna Winton was, she had spirit and a determination of her own that would give him a run for his money...or his child. "Let's go for a drive," Blake suggested.

She looked surprised. "Now?"

"Yes, right now. We can stop and get something for an early supper."

"Jenna..." Rafe warned.

Moving closer to her lawyer, she put her hand

on his arm. "It's all right, Rafe. Really. I'm sure Mr....Blake doesn't have anything underhanded up his sleeve. After all, you're a witness that he's asking me to supper. I promise I won't sign or agree to anything without consulting you."

Looking unhappy with the whole idea, Rafe asked, "Do you have your cell phone?"

She blushed. "No. It wasn't charged so I left it in the apartment."

"I *do* have a cell phone." Blake dislodged it from his belt and handed it to Jenna. "You take this. Apparently Mr. Pierson thinks you may have to send out a mayday."

With a shake of her head, Jenna returned the phone to him. "I'm pregnant, gentlemen—not incapable of looking after myself or using my common sense."

Blake almost smiled and knew he was right about Jenna not being fragile.

Rafe plowed his hand through his hair. "I can't talk you out of this?"

"No, but just to make you feel better, I'll call you when I get back."

"I understand she's pregnant, Pierson," Blake assured her attorney. "I won't take any chances with her or with my baby."

"All right," Rafe finally decided. "But there's just one more thing before you go. Jenna, can I see you privately for a few minutes?"

Seeing that Pierson was obviously Jenna's friend as well as her lawyer, Blake knew when to let well enough alone. "I'll tell Schlessinger and the others that the meeting is concluded for today. I'll be back in a few minutes."

* * *

Fifteen minutes later, Jenna sat beside Blake in his Lexus feeling nervous and unsettled. Maybe this wasn't a good idea after all. There was something about Blake Winston that made her feel electrified. When he'd touched her in the parking lot...

Blake hadn't spoken much but instead switched on the CD player. She supposed the music was supposed to relax her. It was instrumental—piano, violins and guitar that at any other time she might have enjoyed. But as the man beside her glanced over at her, she knew she had to make conversation. She knew she had to figure out what she was doing here with him.

"Where are we going?" she asked.

"I'm heading for the Delta. My boat's there."

"Your boat?"

"It's a cabin cruiser. I thought we might take it out."

"I've never been on a boat before. What if I get seasick?"

He smiled at her. "If you do, I'll bring it back to the marina. Nothing else on earth is as relaxing as being out on the water."

"You think being relaxed is going to help us?"

"It won't hurt. Don't you think better when you're relaxed?"

She didn't know if he was teasing or not. "I've never considered it."

He laughed at that and she liked the sound. It was rich and deep, like his voice.

"What was the last-minute advice Pierson gave you?"

She could see no harm in passing on Rafe's warning. "He warned me not to tell you too much about anything. He doesn't want me to inadvertently help you make your position stronger."

Blake's mouth tightened and his jaw set. As he pulled up to a red light, he turned to look at her. "How long have you and Pierson been friends?"

"About three years. His wife, Shannon, is a psychologist. I consulted with her about one of my students."

"He seems to be as much of a friend as a lawyer."

"He is. He and Shannon were both terrific through everything…everything that happened." Although Shannon had children to care for—Janine, Rafe's daughter whom she'd adopted, and Amelia, the child she and Rafe had had together—she'd been the best friend Jenna could have ever had. When B.J. was in the hospital, Shannon had dropped by often and encouraged Jenna to eat and go for walks to maintain her own health. After B.J. died, Shannon and Rafe invited her to the ranch every weekend. She didn't know what she would have done without them.

"How long was your husband ill?"

When she hesitated, Blake frowned. "Jenna, I'm a security expert. This is information I can access easily."

"You can access medical records? I thought they were supposed to be confidential."

"Any computer specialist can find out exactly what he wants to know. Most private investigators can now, too."

"Because you can do it yourself, you wouldn't have to resort to hiring one of those, though. Right?"

Her temper had a terrifically long fuse, but Blake had just activated it. Maybe everything Rafe Pierson had suspected about him was true. "In fact," she added, "I bet you already know all about me and you just want to see how honest I am with what I tell you.

Maybe this little ride is a mistake. Maybe we should turn back right now."

Finally Blake said, "I do know a few things about you. I'd like to know more, including what kind of mother you'd be. I won't find that out by doing a background check."

"Why do I suddenly feel as if I have to pass some kind of test?"

Without another word, Blake pressed his foot to the brake and pulled his car to the side of the road. "If we go back now, our lawyers are going to fight this out, probably in court. Is that what you want?"

She finally realized why Blake had suggested this drive. If they went about this with lawyers and paperwork, they'd do it mechanically, seeing facts and figures, not the person they were dealing with. What good would that do either of them?

"No, that's not what I want," she murmured.

"Does that mean I shouldn't turn around?"

Looking into his gray eyes, she sensed what a ruthless man he could be. In her case, though, he was making her face what was best for both of them. "I don't want you to turn around, but I don't know if I'm too thrilled about going out on your boat, either."

His gaze was still locked to hers when he nodded. "Fair enough. We can get supper from the marina's deli and eat on the deck. Afterward, you can decide if you want to venture onto the water."

"Fair enough," she repeated, knowing she'd have to stand her ground with this man, knowing she'd have to be careful what she did, what she said and what she felt.

When they stopped at the deli, Blake insisted on buying everything. Since she wasn't really hungry and her stomach was tied up in knots, she simply pointed to a turkey sandwich and let him purchase that for her. He didn't stop with the sandwich order, though, but added fruit salad, rice pudding and an assortment of cookies for dessert. A few minutes later, she followed him to his covered berth and saw immediately that his cabin cruiser, the *Suncatcher,* was much more than a boat to take out on weekends. He could easily live on it.

Blake boarded first, and the step down was a large one.

"I could lift you down," he said with a mischievous gleam in his eyes.

"If you just give me your hand, I think I'll be fine." She didn't know any other way to do it safely, and she wasn't about to let him scoop her up into his arms— as if a man would do that in this day and age.

He was standing close to the step. "Use my shoulder to lean on, too."

Dismay coursed through her when she realized that would help. She wasn't about to take a chance on falling. When she clasped his shoulder, she could feel the strength there, the hard muscles beneath his knit shirt. This little excursion seemed suddenly altogether too intimate. Still, it was too late to back out now.

When she seemed at a loss for a moment, Blake took her hand and she quickly made the descent into the boat. Hoping to put distance between them again, she moved across the deck, examining its cushioned captain's chairs, burled walnut fittings, and conveniences she'd only imagined could *be* on a boat. Suddenly she realized she wasn't going to get much distance from Blake here.

Although he'd released her hand moments before,

she still felt the tautness of his skin. His heat seemed to be part of her now.

He motioned to one of the chairs. "Make yourself comfortable. I'll get plates and silverware and cups in the galley." Then he disappeared down the stairs before she could tell him she could drink her lemonade out of the carton.

"You've really never been on a boat before?" Blake asked her fifteen minutes later as they shared supper and gazed out over the water.

She found herself watching him as he ate. He was obviously hungry, as he downed a twelve-inch sub. When he licked mayonnaise from a finger, she found herself watching his lips. They were sensual, mobile, as fascinating as the gray of his eyes.

Giving herself a mental shake, she realized he'd asked her a question. "No, I've never been on a boat."

"So…what do you think?" he asked with a half smile.

"It's nice," she said. "Sort of like an outdoor restaurant."

After he laughed out loud at that, he said, "I've never heard it put quite that way before. Would you like a tour? There are two bedrooms, a galley and the head downstairs. That's the bathroom."

"That term I'm familiar with. I've never been on a boat, but I've read about them. Still, I don't think I'll need a tour. It doesn't sound as if I'd get lost using the bathroom."

"Afraid to go below with me?"

He was much too perceptive for her own good. These quarters were close enough. "Of course not. But I imagine it's hot down there…"

"I have air-conditioning I can flip on." Finished

with his sandwich now, he leaned forward, his knees almost touching hers. "I'm sorry if I make you nervous."

She was sure she was blushing now. "It's just this whole situation," she said honestly.

"Help me understand," he requested quietly.

Not sure he *could* understand, she still attempted to explain. "Discussing artificial insemination with someone other than my husband and doctor isn't something I've done before. Now a whole gaggle of people are talking about it. I'm a minister's daughter, for heaven's sake. I still don't swear in front of my father or anyone who would carry stories to him. I have to talk to him about all of this, and I don't know how I'm going to do it. On top of that, I've driven off with a strange man against my lawyer's advice. There isn't anyone here within shouting distance and..." She trailed off, not knowing how to explain the rest. She certainly wasn't going to tell him she felt things when she looked at him, especially when he got too close.

After studying her for a full two heartbeats, Blake leaned back as if to give her a little space.

"Why would it be so hard to explain all this to your father even if he is a minister?"

"Dad's very...conservative. He didn't agree with my decision to become artificially inseminated. He insists that if I was supposed to be pregnant with B.J.'s child, it would have happened before he died."

"From the background info I read on you, I saw that your mother died when your brother was a year old. You were nine then?"

It bothered her to think he'd accessed information about her so easily. But now she had to make it more than mere words to him. "Yes, I was nine. So I've always been more like a mother to Gary than a sister."

"Did you take care of your father, too?"

"No. We always had a full-time housekeeper-secretary who cooked and baby-sat."

"I imagine being a minister's daughter is rough."

She shrugged. "Not having a mother was rough. Fortunately I wasn't the wild type to begin with."

When she mentioned not having a mother, she thought she saw a shadow cross Blake's face.

After he took a few swallows of soda, he asked, "How about your brother? Is *he* the wild type?"

"Not really. Gary has just always hated Fawn Grove. We left Pasadena and moved here when he was two. He has his eye on bigger things than a small community can give him. Rafe told me you've been back in Fawn Grove for three years. Do you intend to stay?"

"I intend to make it my home base. It was my home when I was a kid, but I'm in Sacramento more than I'm in Fawn Grove. I travel to L.A. and Seattle a lot, too. There's a charter service I use that makes traveling efficient."

"We lead very different lives," Jenna said softly as she thought about his boat and mansion, flying off to another city at the drop of a hat.

"What are you thinking, Jenna?" he asked, his gaze steady on hers.

Again she was chagrined that he could read her so well. She remembered what Rafe had said about not telling this man too much, and yet she had to follow her instincts. "I'm thinking that you can give this child a lot of advantages I can't, and how a court would look at that."

"In other words, you think I have the upper hand."

"No. You may have money, and maybe you can hire the best nannies there are in this world, but I'm this child's mother. Not by accident, but because I wanted this baby. I think that will pretty much balance the scales unless you resort to something underhanded."

"You're not afraid to pitch straight, are you?" he asked, a bit wryly.

"I might be merely a second-grade teacher, and I might live a simpler life than you do, but I'll fight for this child with every breath inside of me."

Neither of them spoke for a full minute. Finally he stood and she did the same so he wouldn't tower over her any more than he already did.

"Round one is over," he concluded. "I think we both established that neither of us is going to sign away our parental rights."

"What do we do about round two?"

After studying her for a few moments, he eased one hand into his pocket. "I think we should take an intermission before we jump into the ring again. How about that boat ride?"

"You're serious?"

"I didn't bring you to the Delta to sit on the deck and rock in the ripples. I think you're more fearless than that."

He had her pegged wrong this time. She wasn't fearless at all. She was afraid he'd somehow manage to take this baby away from her. She was afraid she'd forget B.J.'s face. She was afraid that Blake Winston could be too persuasive when he set his mind to be. Yet she wouldn't let him see the fear because that would definitely be giving him the upper hand.

"All right," she agreed. "Take me for a boat ride.

But I'll warn you right now, I'm pregnant and I just ate supper.''

At that, he chuckled and shook his head. ''I'll consider myself warned. Stay right there and I'll get your life jacket.''

Blake made sure Jenna had safely returned from the bathroom and was comfortable on the deck before he took the helm. She held on to the arms of the captain's chair as the boat moved away from the slip and onto the river. After a few minutes, she began to relax...if that was at all possible under the circumstances.

Jenna watched as they passed all the Sacramento marinas. Then the boat picked up speed, and she felt as if she were on a cruise. The blue sky, the hum of the engine, the sun and the warm breeze made her realize she'd never had an experience quite like this. She could see why Blake was drawn to the water. It was peaceful out here in a way that nothing else could be peaceful.

It seemed only a short while later when Blake dropped anchor in a cove and descended the stairs to the deck. ''I thought you might like to take it all in from a different vantage point. I know you don't feel free to walk around while we're moving.''

He was right about that. She'd almost fallen asleep in the comfortable chair and had been content there. Standing, she stretched, all the while aware of Blake as he stood at the rail looking far down the river. His shoulders were so broad, his skin tanned, his body fit. A tingle of excitement rushed through her as she went to stand at the rail beside him, making sure their elbows didn't touch, reminding herself Blake only wanted something from her—his child.

Taking his phone from his belt, he handed it to her.

"Why don't you call Pierson. It's almost five and I'm sure he's probably ready to put out an APB on you."

As she glanced at her watch, she realized it was indeed five o'clock. She couldn't believe they'd been on the water for an hour. He was probably right about Rafe being worried. As she punched in the number, she asked, "This will work here?"

"There's a tower not far away on the shoreline. While I'm out, I often duck in here to make a few calls."

Walking over to the bench seat, she gazed out at the horizon. Rafe's receptionist answered on the second ring and then patched her through.

"Rafe, it's Jenna."

"I was beginning to get worried. How was your drive?"

"Um...it's not over yet. I'm out on Blake's boat."

There was silence. "Jenna, do you know what you're doing?"

"Not exactly." She glanced at Blake and saw he was watching her.

"Do you know how unorthodox this is? You shouldn't be fraternizing with him if we're thinking about going to court."

If they did go to court, who was going to pay those bills? She didn't want to say that and have Blake overhear. "We'll talk about it when I see you."

"I'll be in court all day tomorrow."

"Then I'll talk to you on Thursday."

She heard his heavy sigh. "You can be as stubborn as Shannon."

"I'll take that as a compliment."

"Call me tonight when you get home."

"Rafe..."

"Call me, Jenna."

"All right. But don't let the rest of your hair turn gray over this. I'm fine. In fact, it's very peaceful out here."

"The calm before the storm," her lawyer muttered.

A few minutes later she stretched out her arm to give Blake his phone. His fingers brushed over hers as he took it, and she again felt guilt as something besides the baby stirred inside of her, something she hadn't even felt with B.J.

Still trying to absorb the tingling jolt of awareness that had rushed through her at the brush of his skin on hers, she peered into the distance, trying to see the future, trying to see her life without B.J. but with Blake Winston's child. It was unfathomable, as deeply hidden as any buried treasure.

"Do you have other children?" she suddenly asked Blake.

His brows arched. "No, I don't. I've never been married, either, if you're wondering about that."

There was an edge to his voice, and she realized he didn't like personal questions. "You know a whole lot more about me than I know about you."

The tension seemed to leave his brow as he turned his back to the railing and faced her. "I don't have any other children because I've always been careful."

She needed to ask the most personal question of all and felt awkward doing it. Yet the answer was more important than her discomfort. "Why did you have your sperm frozen?"

At first she thought he wasn't going to answer her, that he'd go right back up those stairs and pilot them back to the marina. But then he said, "I'd heard that men's sperm become less potent as they age. Since a serious relationship isn't in the cards for me, I decided I'd hire a surrogate and have a baby after I was forty. Freezing my sperm seemed like the practical thing to do.''

She felt as if she'd landed in a minefield. There were so many questions she wanted to ask, yet from the expression on his face, she knew he wouldn't answer them.

"I suppose everyone tries to plan their future and very few succeed," she mused. "It never quite goes the way we expect, does it?"

"Fate has thrown its share of boomerangs at me," he admitted, as though he was telling her something he wouldn't tell many others.

Being on this boat with him created intimacy that scared her. Maybe it was the way he was looking at her, maybe it was the sparks of silver in his gray eyes, maybe it was the way they were standing almost toe to toe.

Slowly he reached out and fingered a tendril of her hair that wisped along her cheek. Waves of heat seemed to undulate between them. "You're a very beautiful woman, Jenna."

She felt her cheeks go hot for many reasons, mostly because she'd never thought of herself in those terms. "I'm pregnant," she said, as if that contradicted him.

His crooked half smile made her tummy flip-flop. "I think being pregnant has just added to your beauty."

She was twenty-six, but she felt like a naive teenager with this man.

"I'm glad you came along with me today." His voice was husky and as mesmerizing as his eyes.

She didn't know if it was the sway of the boat or the force of the breeze, or something else entirely, but she felt herself leaning toward him. As he began to bend his head, the call of a gull startled her and she was totally dismayed at what she'd almost let happen.

Stepping away from Blake, she tried to slow her racing pulse. "I think we'd better go back."

He didn't look at all flustered, and she wondered if his tender touch had been planned along with everything else this afternoon. Was this why Rafe had been fearful for her? Had he been afraid she'd come under Blake Winston's spell?

That wasn't going to happen. She had her child to think about.

Turning away from Blake, she went over to the captain's chair again and settled into it, waiting for him to take her back to the marina. When she returned to Fawn Grove, she'd call Rafe and then they'd plan a strategy. This man would not take her baby away from her.

She wouldn't let him.

Chapter Three

As Blake parked behind Jenna's apartment complex, he was bothered by the silence between them. It had seemed to drown out the music coming from the CD player during the drive back. For that one moment on the boat, he'd forgotten about their situation, about who he was and who she was, and that they might be headed to court. It had been a stupid impulse to even *think* about kissing her. He had practically everything a man could want. Yet Jenna Winton made him long for more.

Climbing out of his car, he closed the door and walked around to the passenger side. He knew better than to expect loyalty from a woman. He knew better than to expect anything but physical satisfaction from a relationship. Danielle Howard had taught him a valuable lesson when he was eighteen, and he'd never forgotten it. Her betrayal had pushed him toward the success he'd found. If only his father had lived to see it...if only his father had had the courage to wait for Blake to return...the courage to keep on living even when he thought his life was over.

As Jenna unfastened her seat belt and opened her door, it seemed natural to hold out his hand to her. She didn't take it. As easily as any woman who wasn't pregnant, she swung her legs to the pavement and stood with a dancer's grace.

"I'll walk you to your apartment," he said after he closed her door.

"That's not necessary."

"I want to make sure you're safely inside before I leave." He wouldn't mind having another look around her place. If she did get custody and brought his child home to her apartment...

He couldn't let her have custody. He wouldn't give up his baby. Whether he'd known it or not, for years he'd needed some connection...some bond. He knew he'd spoil a child, but he wanted his kid to have every advantage he'd never had.

"What are you thinking about?" she asked as they walked toward the building's outside entrance.

Her question wasn't one that was asked often. His employees and business associates usually knew exactly what was on his mind. "Why?" he returned warily.

"You looked so fierce."

"I was thinking about the baby—what I could give him...or her." As they started up the stairs, he asked, "Have you had a sonogram?"

She glanced at him. "Yes, but I didn't want to know the sex. I wanted to be surprised."

That was a way they were very different. He didn't

like surprises. "That makes shopping difficult, doesn't it? You'd have to buy everything in green or yellow."

"I haven't started shopping yet," she said quietly.

"Why not?"

They'd reached the landing when she answered, "Superstition, I guess. I just wanted to make sure everything was all right. I wanted to make sure I was really going to term with the baby."

He took her arm. "Is there something wrong I don't know about?"

"No. No! I just felt more comfortable waiting. Besides, Shannon told me there are good baby sales at the beginning of July."

Thinking about what he'd learned of Jenna's finances and the stringent budget she must be following, he wondered if she even had a room set up for the baby. "How many bedrooms do you have in your apartment?"

"Just one. But I'm going to breast-feed so I'll have the baby in my room with me, anyway."

With her words, his gaze dropped to her breasts. He found himself picturing—

Blanking out the image, he motioned to the hall entrance to guide her ahead of him. As they walked down the second-floor hall, Blake saw two other apartment doors were open—probably because of the problem with the air-conditioning. If there was a breeze, the residents were trying to pull it through.

An exotic-looking woman who appeared to be near forty came to the door when she saw Jenna pass. "Jenna," she said fondly. Her hair was fixed on the top of her head with a yellow banana barrette, her cut-offs were short, and her stretch top barely contained her breasts.

Jenna greeted her neighbor with a smile and a wave. "Hi, Ramona. Staying cool?"

"I've been sharing Trina's Popsicles. Want one?" The orange treat in question dripped onto her hand.

"No, thanks. I just want to get a cold shower and turn in."

Blake asked, "Any word on when the air-conditioning will be fixed?"

Ramona looked him up and down appraisingly. Apparently liking what she saw, she smiled. "Not any time soon. The landlord said he's waiting for a part. You know how that goes. By the way, Jenna, you have a visitor."

Jenna stilled. "A visitor?"

"I didn't want you to get a heart attack when you walked into your apartment. Your father's there."

"Do you know why?"

With a shrug, Ramona shook her head. "I dunno. When I saw him using his key, he just said something about not being able to get hold of you."

Jenna looked chagrined. But then her expression eased again as she asked her neighbor, "Did he say anything about another counseling session?"

"No. I made sure he knew Joe was gone for good. I took Trina to church on Sunday and your dad seemed pleased. I owe him a lot. He wants Trina and me to stay safe. I want that, too."

"You haven't heard from Joe since you sent him packing, have you?"

"Nope. Word has it he's in San Francisco. I don't know why I let him treat me like I did. If it wasn't for you sending me to your dad, I might have ended up with more than a few bruises." As if she was embarrassed by her admission, she asked with a wink, "You been out on a date?"

Flustered, Jenna glanced at Blake. "Oh, no. No. Just business."

"Uh-huh," Ramona drawled with a wicked smile. "Looks to me, you know how to pick 'em."

When Jenna turned beet red, Blake felt sorry for her. "Business" didn't quite cover why he was here. Still, he rescued her. "Maybe we'd better see what your father wants." He was curious about Jenna's father and welcomed the opportunity to meet him.

Obviously relieved by his cue, Jenna said to her neighbor, "Give Trina a good-night kiss for me."

"Will do." Ramona was still smiling as she turned and went back into her apartment.

"She's a friend of yours?" Blake asked, surprised.

"Ramona's been terrific. I've had morning sickness on and off throughout the pregnancy. When she doesn't hear me up and about, she knocks on the bathroom wall. It's thin and we can talk through it. She can check on me that way."

"Her husband was violent?"

"Joe was her boyfriend. Whenever he got drunk…" Jenna shook her head. "It was a bad situation. But after dad counseled her, she finally did what she had to do to protect her daughter."

As Blake and Jenna stood outside her apartment door, he asked, "Why would your father be here?"

"He probably just wants to make sure I'm all right."

Blake could certainly understand that feeling. He'd felt protective about Jenna as soon as he learned she was carrying his baby.

The table lamp beside the sofa was glowing when they stepped inside her apartment.

Jenna's father eyed Blake suspiciously as he stood and approached her. "Where have you been? I've been worried sick."

Glancing at Blake, she looked embarrassed. "I spent the afternoon with Mr. Winston." She motioned toward him. "Blake, this is my father, Reverend Charles Seabring."

Reverend Seabring looked Blake up and down again. "I've seen your picture in the paper, haven't I? You own a security company and have very..." He hesitated, then continued, "Important clients."

Unfortunately, Blake often did make the newspapers, usually coming away from a charity event with a tall blonde on his arm. He knew he had a reputation for being a jet-setting bachelor who never intended to settle down. That image hadn't bothered him before. Now he knew the reverend would disapprove of any time his daughter might spend with Blake. "My company's based in Sacramento and, yes, sometimes I am in the papers. I understand you're a minister?"

"Yes, I am. I should be preparing my sermon for Sunday, but I was too distracted by visions of my daughter lying in a ditch somewhere. Why didn't you answer your cell phone?"

Squaring her shoulders, she stood up to him. "Because I didn't have it with me. I forgot to charge it last night and I was in a hurry when I left today."

"I got that phone for you so you'd have it in an emergency. That means you have to keep it with you."

Apparently Jenna had had enough of her father's protective streak. Spots of color appeared on her cheeks. "I'm twenty-six, Dad. You told me that cell phone was a gift and that's why I took it. But if it comes with strings, you can have it back. I'm not going to report in to you three times a day.''

Her father ran his hand through his thinning and graying brown hair and finally smiled. ''I suppose once a day is too much to ask?''

Her expression softened. ''Once a day is fine. I would have called you within the next half hour.''

Charles peered at Blake with a penetrating gaze that Blake recognized. Danielle Howard's father had looked at him in just the same way with a mixture of fatherly disapproval and righteousness that still angered him.

''I suppose your evening with Mr. Winston isn't over yet?'' he asked Jenna.

''We have a few things to discuss,'' she replied softly.

Blake could see Charles Seabring was dying to ask what, but he didn't. Blake was sure if Jenna had been a few years younger, *he* would be the one who was leaving first.

''I see,'' Seabring said. ''Will you stop by the parsonage tomorrow?''

''I told you I would. Shirley's going to go over everything with me so I'll know what to do when she leaves. I'll stop in for breakfast with you and Gary first. All right?''

Her father nodded. ''I'll tell Shirley to make those apple pancakes you like so much. Eight-thirty too early for you?''

''Eight-thirty's fine.'' Jenna walked her father to the door, and at the threshold she gave him a kiss on the cheek. When he didn't hug her as most fathers would have, Blake decided that the minister wasn't a demonstrative man.

Two minutes later, Jenna had closed the door and leaned against it, sighing heavily.

"Those apple pancakes come with a price, I bet," Blake remarked. "Your father's going to give you the third degree tomorrow, isn't he?"

"Most likely."

She looked so troubled, Blake wanted to take her hand. Vetoing that thought, he asked, "Does he know this baby isn't your husband's?" He didn't like using that term, but he didn't know what else to say.

"Not yet. *I'm* still trying to absorb it. Dad was so against the insemination in the first place. This is going to really throw him." She shook her head. "I'm afraid it will put more distance between us."

"Has the distance always been there?" Blake asked gently. He thought about his own father, the distance between them. After his mother's death when Blake was twelve, his dad had pulled away from life and drowned his grief in a bottle of gin. Then, Blake hadn't understood his father's self-pity and sadness. He himself had dealt with the grief by playing sports harder, boxing a friend's punching bag and studying late into the night. He and his dad had grown farther and farther apart. Everything had been unsaid for years...so much that should have been said before his father committed suicide. If they'd been able to talk...if Blake had stayed in Fawn Grove and made his father get help...or if he'd returned sooner...

"I can't remember if Dad was different before my mother died," Jenna answered, pulling Blake back to the here and now. "I seem to remember that he was warmer, not so serious. But afterward, it was as if he pulled the shutters closed and turned inward. And after we moved here..."

"Why did your dad move here?"

"He said he wanted Gary and me to grow up away from hustle and bustle of city life. He was pastor of a much larger congregation in Pasadena."

When she came closer to Blake, she apologized, "I'm sorry if he was a bit rude to you. I didn't know quite how to handle our being together today. He's never seen me with any man but B.J. And it's not as if we *are* together."

She was enchantingly shy and altogether out of her depth. This time he *did* take her hand. "Jenna, I know we really haven't worked out anything today. But I'd like you to think about joint custody."

He saw the anguish on her face at the thought of not having her baby all the time, and he knew the same turmoil. If he was going to be a father, he really wanted to be a father twenty-four hours a day, seven days a week. He'd never been committed to anything but his work, yet now he wanted to be committed to this baby. Everything he'd always worked for suddenly seemed to have a purpose.

"There isn't going to be an easy solution to this, and I think you know that. So think about joint custody, all right?" he suggested again.

When she nodded, he could see how tormented she was by the idea, but he couldn't do anything about that.

After she walked him to the door, they stood there in silence. He didn't really want to go, but he knew he didn't have a good reason to stay. "I'll call you." Taking a business card from the pocket of his slacks, he handed it to her. "Or you can call me. The cell phone number will get you through immediately. I never turn it off."

She gave him a weak little smile. "Or let it go un-charged."

He grinned. "Once in a while I forget."

"I think you're just trying to make me feel better. You're the kind of man who never forgets anything," she murmured.

"One afternoon and you think you have a handle on my character?" He was partly joking, partly serious.

"I don't know about a handle on your character, but I think I've gotten to know a few things about you just as you've gotten to know a few things about me—a lot more about me. Rafe's not going to be happy about that."

"We have to find a way clear for us that's going to be good for this baby, no matter what Pierson or my lawyer think."

"I know that," she said. "You should have my cell phone number, too."

"Tell me. I'll remember it."

Jenna's forehead was damp from the heat, her cheeks still rosy as she rattled it off, and he committed it to memory. His physical response to her wasn't anything he understood. Maybe away from her he could figure it out.

Opening the door, he asked, "When are you going to tell your father about this?"

"When the time is right."

Gazing into her velvety brown eyes, he wondered how she was going to know. He wanted to take the kiss he hadn't taken on the boat. He wanted to hold her and let her rest her head against his shoulder. He wanted his child…and that might or might not have anything to do with Jenna.

"Take care of yourself," he said, his voice husky.

Then he left, before needing and wanting and longing took him back more years than he wanted to count.

When Jenna let herself in the back door of the parsonage the following morning, it was a little after eight and Shirley was already busy in the kitchen. Her father's secretary and housekeeper was in her late fifties. Her black hair was streaked with gray now and cut in a short hairdo that looked easy to maintain. She wore navy slacks and a paisley blouse this morning with an apron tied around her waist.

"It smells good in here," Jenna said. The back screen door closed behind her.

"I'm so glad you're joining your dad for breakfast. He's on the phone in his office. I'm not sure Gary's up yet."

Jenna suspected Shirley had had feelings for her father for many years. But she never let them show, and Jenna didn't even know for sure if her dad had noticed his secretary was interested in him. "As soon as Gary smells food, he'll be here."

Shirley laughed. "You're right about that. How are you feeling?"

"I'm still having trouble with the nausea now and then, but other than that, I'm feeling great."

Gary came into the kitchen then, dressed in jeans and a red T-shirt, his dark brown hair tousled as if he hadn't combed it. "Hey, sis. I didn't know you were coming to breakfast. What's the special occasion?"

"No special occasion. I just thought I'd take advantage of Shirley's cooking before she leaves for a few days."

"I forgot about that. Dad and I are going to be eating a lot of fast food."

"I've put enough casseroles in the freezer to last until Tuesday. You won't starve. In fact, I doubt if your father will even miss me."

Jenna wondered if Gary heard the wistfulness in Shirley's voice, too.

Her brother was already pouring himself a glass of juice. "Are you still going to help me with that video project tonight?" he asked Jenna.

Picking that moment to walk into the kitchen, their father asked, "What video project?"

Gary's goal in life was to become a movie director. Their dad disapproved of the idea and did everything he could to squelch it. But Gary had boundless enthusiasm when it came to using a secondhand camcorder he'd saved for and bought when he was ten.

"It's for that extra class I'm taking this summer," he said patiently.

"I thought you were taking a history course."

"It is. I can do a paper or something more innovative on the history of Fawn Grove. I'm going to do a video. But I want to brainstorm with Jenna for the best ideas for scenes. It sure beats doing a research paper."

Her father sat down at the head of the table.

"I can use this video when I apply to film school," Gary added, as if testing the water again on the subject.

"You're not applying to film school. We've discussed this."

"No, we haven't discussed it. You told me what you thought. You didn't listen to what *I* thought."

Though Jenna gave Gary a warning glance, he didn't heed it. "So what time tonight, sis?"

"You have to trim the hedge," her father reminded his son.

"What time do you get off work today?" Jenna

asked gently. Her brother was working at the local grocery store for the summer.

"I'll be off at five-thirty, but till I do the trimming, take a shower, get something to eat…"

"Why don't you come over to the apartment around seven-thirty? If the air-conditioning still isn't fixed, we'll go for ice cream and talk there."

"Sounds good to me."

While Jenna and Gary had been working out their plans, Shirley had delivered plates of pancakes, bacon and scrambled eggs to the table. Untying her apron, she said to Jenna, "Just come into the office when you're through and we'll get started."

"I'd like to have a word with my daughter first," Charles said, eyeing Jenna.

She should have known she wouldn't be able to escape without the third degree Blake had warned her about. She glanced at Shirley. "I'm sure it won't take long."

She wouldn't let it take long. She wasn't ready to tell her father that this baby belonged to Blake Winston. Although she'd seen the censure in her dad's eyes last night at the idea she'd spent time with a man like Blake, she wasn't going to give him any further information or food for more thought. This was her life and she'd make decisions on her own. In the meantime—

"Shirley, why don't you sit down and join us for breakfast?" Jenna prompted.

The woman looked shocked. "Oh, I couldn't do that."

"Why not? Did you already eat breakfast?"

"Well, no. I just grabbed a banana before I came over here this morning, like I usually do."

"You made this wonderful food and we're certainly

not going to eat it all. Come on, join us. Don't you think she should, Dad?''

Gary gave her a what-are-you-up-to-now look.

Charles glanced at Shirley, then Jenna. ''If you didn't have breakfast, Shirley, you should eat something. As Jenna said, there's plenty here.''

It wasn't an enthusiastic invitation, but it wasn't a dismissal of the idea, either. Shirley must have realized that, too, because she gave Charles her broadest smile. ''Thank you for asking. I'd like to join all of you.''

After she pulled an extra dish from the cupboard and took silverware from the drawer, she sat around the corner from Charles, next to Gary, and loaded up her plate.

After breakfast, fortunately Jenna was able to evade her father's questions about Blake. He'd just asked her what kind of business she'd had with Winston when he got a call from a member of his congregation that he had to take. After the call, he told Shirley and Jenna he had to go to the hospital. The look he gave his daughter said they'd return to their discussion later. By then, maybe she'd know what to tell him and be able to explain what had happened at the clinic.

Around eleven, after she and Shirley finished their to-do list, Jenna found herself at loose ends. Needing someone she could talk to and trust about her predicament, she drove out to the Rocky R, hoping Shannon would be free. During the summer, the psychologist lessened her client load and let her partner handle most of it so she could spend more time with her daughters, Janine and Amelia.

The Rocky R was about fifteen minutes outside of Fawn Grove. A wooden archway welcomed Jenna as she drove her car up the lane to the house. Marianne,

Shannon's partner, was working in the corral with a student.

Jenna parked in the gravel area near the two-story house and was relieved to see Shannon's truck there, too. Her aunt Cora's car was gone, though, and that could mean Shannon wouldn't be home, either.

As Jenna ascended the porch steps, she could see that the front door was open. She rang the bell and called, "Anyone home?"

Shannon came to the door dressed in her usual jeans and a blue-and-yellow-plaid, short-sleeved shirt. She was all smiles when she saw Jenna. "Hi, there. I just came in from grooming the horses and washed up. I'm about ready to fix lunch. You want some?"

"Are the girls here?"

Holding open the wooden screen door, she explained, "They went into town with Cora to get groceries. They should be back any minute."

"This isn't just a friendly visit," Jenna said as she stepped inside. "I need perspective on everything that's happened, and I thought you could give it to me."

"I'll do my best. Let's talk in the kitchen while I make salads."

Shannon's kitchen was bright, colorful and welcoming. "Has Rafe told you anything?" Jenna asked her friend.

"He can't. Confidentiality between lawyer and client. I only know what you told me after your first meeting at the clinic about the baby not being B.J.'s. Rafe paced most of last evening but wouldn't tell me why. Did that have something to do with you?"

"I...I was with Blake Winston yesterday against Rafe's advice. Blake thought if we went off somewhere and talked without lawyers, it might make everything easier.''

Shannon gave Jenna her full attention. ''Did it?''

She felt her cheeks grow warm. ''I don't know. He's so— I don't know how to explain it. He's just so much a…man.''

Shannon seemed surprised at that and her lips twitched up. ''What does *that* mean?''

As Jenna sank into one of the kitchen chairs at the table, she thought about it, then tried to put those thoughts into words. ''He's so confident but he doesn't talk much about himself. He's used to getting his own way and giving orders, but yet he seemed to know how to listen, too.''

''It sounds to me as if you learned a lot about him in one afternoon.''

''He learned a lot more about me. When I told Rafe that last night, he wasn't happy. But I had to be honest with Blake.''

''Do you think he was honest with you?''

''I think everything he told me was true. From what I gathered, this child means a lot to him. He had his sperm frozen so one day he could hire a surrogate. Apparently he wanted his sperm to be fully potent—'' Jenna stopped, feeling a bit embarrassed.

Shannon's brows arched. ''A man like Blake Winston could have any woman he wanted. I wonder why he planned to use a surrogate?''

''I got the feeling that a serious relationship isn't on his agenda. But he's not your typical confirmed bachelor if he wants to be a daddy. I think he's a very complex man.''

After Shannon was quiet for a few moments, she said, ''Blake Winston knows powerful people, not just actors and actresses, but politicians, too. From what I understand, he's got it all—money, good looks..." She paused before she added, "Charm. A man like that could be very persuasive. Do you think he was *handling* you yesterday?"

"I don't know. I was upset, that was for sure. Yet I didn't feel he was charming me. I mean, I felt he was as thrown off balance by all of this as I've been. When we were out on his boat—"

"Out on his boat?" Shannon cut in.

"He suggested it. He said it was the best place to relax. And it was. It was so peaceful out there, Shannon. Even though I'd never been on a boat, when he was at the helm, I trusted him."

"You like the man."

When she thought about it, she wasn't sure how to explain what she felt around him. "I don't know him yet." Even though Shannon was a good friend, she didn't feel comfortable telling her about being almost kissed, the feelings that had made her tingle all over. They didn't seem any more right today than they had yesterday. She already knew what Shannon would tell her—that B.J. was dead and she had to go on. But up until two days ago, she'd intended to keep B.J.'s memory alive forever by having his child.

"Did he make any offers?"

"I think he might agree to joint custody. But I can't imagine not holding my baby every day, not caring for it every moment."

"Joint custody doesn't have to be half a week at his house, half a week at yours. Courts are willing to be flexible if the two of *you* can be flexible. You have to think about the trauma going to court over this would cause—not only the disruption in your life, but in your child's life. Custody battles usually turn nasty because both sides want the advantage. Rafe can tell you that better than anyone.''

''Do you think I should agree to joint custody?''

''What *I* think doesn't matter, Jenna. You have to solve this in your heart and come up with what you can live with.''

A beep sounded from Jenna's purse and she fished inside for her cell phone. When she answered it, she expected to hear her father's voice…or Gary's. Instead she heard ''Jenna? It's Blake.''

''Oh. Hi.''

''Am I catching you at a bad time?''

She glanced at Shannon. ''No. I was just having lunch with…a friend.''

''I won't keep you. How would you like to come to my house for dinner tonight?''

Dinner with Blake? If she agreed, what tactic would he use tonight to convince her that joint custody was the solution to their dilemma?

Chapter Four

As Jenna drove up the long driveway to Blake's house that evening, she was more nervous than she could ever remember being. She told herself the anxiety came from the unknown, from the fear that Blake would take her baby. Yet if she was honest with herself, it was more than that. Blake Winston unnerved her.

She parked her car along the circular drive in front of the stately stone house, noticing a white luxury sedan parked there, too. Had Blake invited someone else to join them? Did the car belong to his lawyer? Was she walking into a setup?

Checking her purse for her cell phone, she decided she could always call Rafe. She could always leave. She hadn't consulted her lawyer about accepting this invitation, though she knew Shannon would tell him Blake had issued it. For some reason she felt she had to meet Blake Winston on personal terms without the impediments of tables and attorneys and official forms.

After she rang the doorbell, she waited, smoothing the blue-striped rayon of her dress over her tummy. "How are we doing, little one," she asked gently, and smiled. This one-sided conversation would become more than that as soon as her baby was born.

Her baby. Blake's child.

The door was opened by a petite woman wearing a black pantsuit and white apron. Her hair was styled in a close perm around her head and her red lipstick shouted personality. Her blue eyes twinkled when she saw Jenna. "I expect you're Mrs. Winton?"

"Yes, I am."

"Come right in, then. Mr. Winston said I should bring you into the parlor." She stopped walking for a moment and lowered her voice. "I think he's tired of talking politics, and he'd much rather sit down and talk with you." She glanced at Jenna's belly. "I know all about what's going on. I heard Mr. Winston talking to his lawyer." She started walking again.

As the older woman opened a large mahogany door, she said close to Jenna's ear, "My name's Marilyn. Just give a holler if you need anything." Then she moved ahead of Jenna and announced, "Mrs. Winton is here, sir."

As Jenna took a quick glance around, she caught sight of brass lamps and damask lamp shades, a cut-velvet settee in hunter green and peach, heavy draperies the same shade of green. Blake was standing by the marble fireplace. Another gentleman who was sipping a drink appraised her curiously from the camel-leather wing chair.

After a moment, she realized who he was—Nolan Constantine, the mayor of Fawn Grove.

Her gaze sought Blake's. "I'm a little early. I'm sorry if I've interrupted. I can wait out in the foyer...."

Blake moved away from the mantel toward a serving cart. "Don't be silly, Jenna. Nolan and I were finished our discussion. Nolan Constantine, this is Jenna Winton. Jenna, the fine mayor of Fawn Grove. We've been discussing his ambition to reach a higher office, but I think we're both tired of it. What do you think, Nolan?"

Blake's off-white oxford shirt was open at the collar and his khaki slacks were casual. On the other hand, Nolan's styled blond hair, navy suit and red tie made him look as if he were attending a board meeting.

Standing, Nolan placed his drink on the occasional table by his chair. "I think we're finished for now. I have a meeting with Preston Howard tonight. By the way, his daughter Danielle said to say hello. I met her at a fund-raiser last weekend. When I mentioned my plans and the fact that you might be backing me, she said you two were old friends."

A subtle change came over Blake. Jenna couldn't exactly say what it was...maybe more tension in his shoulders, a shadowing of his eyes.

"I didn't know Danielle was back in town," he said to Nolan casually. "Last I heard, she was living on a ranch in Montana with a cattle baron."

"She told me she came back to Fawn Grove a few weeks ago. She's divorced now. I think I made a good impression. What she thinks might carry weight with her father. If he decides to come on board, we'll be all set."

Blake had poured lemonade from a pitcher into an

ice-filled glass and now he took it to Jenna. "Lemonade." Suddenly he frowned. "Or would you rather have milk?"

Jenna told herself she'd imagined the change in him when Danielle Howard's name was mentioned. Yet he was gazing at Jenna now as if there was nothing else on his mind. His gray eyes had such power she couldn't find her voice for a moment, but then she accepted the glass he offered. "Lemonade's fine. Thank you."

Nolan cleared his throat and addressed Blake again. "I have to thank you for seeing me on such short notice. I'll call you tomorrow and let you know how the meeting with Howard went." Stopping in front of Jenna, he added, "It was good to meet you, Mrs. Winton. Have a nice dinner."

He hardly waited for her goodbye before he was out the parlor door.

Blake gave a wry smile. "Nolan has more energy than he knows what to do with. Most people think he's all public persona but there's substance there, too. He'll make a good congressman."

"That's if he wins," she said realistically.

Blake chuckled. "You have a way of bringing a man back to earth."

She felt herself blushing. "I didn't mean you couldn't get him elected."

"I might not be able to. I don't have that much influence, Jenna, in spite of what your lawyer may have told you."

Was he trying to throw her off guard, make her comfortable so she'd let down her defenses?

He nodded to the hall doorway. "Marilyn's going to be serving us dinner on the screened-in porch. Is that all right with you?"

"That sounds lovely."

As they strolled down the hall, Jenna couldn't help peering into some of the rooms. Her gaze snagged on a chandelier in the dining room with a table large enough to sit twelve, at least.

"I thought the porch would be more comfortable than shouting across that table," he teased when he caught her looking.

"It's a wonderful room. You'd never have to worry about enough space for holidays, in-laws, aunts, uncles, grandparents."

He frowned. "I don't have any of those."

"No family?"

"No family."

An awkwardness fell over them that was different from the tension that usually vibrated between them. Trying to break it, she asked on a lighter note, "Where do you usually eat supper?"

"At my desk. And there *is* a smaller dining room for more intimate parties."

She could imagine what those intimate parties would consist of—Blake and a woman sharing lobster and champagne with candlelight flickering.

As they passed yet another room, Blake nodded to the interior. "This is my favorite."

Standing in the doorway, Jenna could see why. There was a floor-to-ceiling brick fireplace, brass and warm wood, a comfortable-looking, wine-and-navy couch and matching recliner. "Even this..." She stopped.

"Even this what?" he asked, studying her.

"Even this room doesn't look lived in. Your house is beautiful, but I can't feel you here." She became embarrassed as soon as she'd said it.

"Feel me here?" He looked intrigued by her comment.

"When B.J. and I bought our house, we made it so very—ours. I picked out a chair, he picked out a lamp. My magazines lay on one side of the sofa, his on the other. His sneakers always sat by the hassock. It always seemed I left a half-finished cup of tea by the arm of the chair. Anyone walking into that house would know immediately B.J. liked to collect old bottles and I stitched crewelwork in the evenings. And the bedroom..." She shook her head. "I never could get B.J. to pick up his socks."

Blake shifted toward her, but although the doorway was large, his arm grazed her tummy. The contact was electrifying, and as her gaze shot to his, she expected to see embarrassment there, too. She should have known better. Apparently Blake Winston didn't embarrass easily.

"When guests stay overnight they don't usually leave anything behind," he remarked, referring to her last comment.

Jenna knew Blake was speaking of the bedroom. She knew he was speaking of women he might take pleasure with for a night, a week or a month. Apparently none of them stayed, or more to the point, he didn't invite any of them to stay. Why was that? Why wasn't he interested in a serious relationship? Why didn't he have any family?

"It was stupid of me to compare our house to yours. It's not the same at all."

"Your house was a home. My house is just a house." Then he thought about it for a moment. "Filling it with a child's laughter could make a big difference."

"Filling any house with a child's laughter makes a big difference." The subject of their child wafted between them and entwined around them like a web binding them tighter. Yet Jenna knew gossamer strands were easily broken, and she and Blake could end up on different sides of a fence that would divide them.

Stepping away from the doorway and into the hall once more, Blake removed himself from their close proximity and she felt herself take a deep breath of relief.

When Blake showed Jenna into the screened-in porch, she saw that it was much more than that. A three-tiered fountain bubbled amid fuchsia-and-white hibiscus. The heels of her sandals clicked on the ceramic-tile floor as she passed screened windows that faced manicured lawns and gardens alive with roses, bougainvillea and citrus. The ceiling fan overhead whirred softly.

Blake motioned to the wicker table and chairs. The blue-and-tan cushioned seats were comfortable, and within moments he was standing behind Jenna, pushing in her chair at a wicker-and-glass table already laden with a fruit tray and assorted breads and salads.

After Marilyn bustled in with platters filled with lemon-pepper chicken, fresh green beans and small parslied potatoes, Jenna took a whiff and smiled. "Do you eat like this all the time?"

Marilyn winked and said in an aside, "He'd eat steak and potatoes every night if I'd let him."

With that announcement, she hurried away from the table and looked over her shoulder before leaving the room. "Strawberry shortcake for dessert."

"She's been my housekeeper for the past ten years,"

Blake said with a rueful smile. "And is never afraid to offer her opinion."

"She sounds more like a friend than a house-keeper."

"Maybe she is. She doesn't have any family, either. So I guess we sort of look after each other." He paused and added, "I know I can trust her. I can't say that with confidence with most of the other people I deal with."

That statement was revealing, and it was the first real piece of Blake that Jenna had seen.

Once he was seated, he got to the point of his invitation to dinner. "I asked you here to talk about joint custody," he said honestly.

She took a deep breath and swallowed. "To consider joint custody, I have to know more about you. I can't just—" She'd laid her purse on the chair beside her and now her cell phone beeped from inside.

"Go ahead and answer it," he said with a nod of his jaw. "I don't mind."

She rarely got calls on her cell phone so she decided not to ignore it. Reaching into her bag, she pulled the phone out and answered it.

"Hey, sis, did you forget about me?"

"Gary!" How could she have forgotten about the meeting with her brother? After she'd gotten the call from Blake with his invitation to dinner, she hadn't been able to think about much else. When she'd left Shannon's, she'd stopped at a baby store and looked at all the pretty things, not even considering her plans with Gary for tonight.

"I'm so sorry. Where are you?"

"At the pay phone up the street from your apart-ment. Where are *you*?"

"I'm having dinner with...a friend."

"Blake Winston?" Gary asked. "I heard you and Dad talking about him before he got called out. Who *is* this guy, anyway?"

That's what she was trying to find out. "It's complicated." She glanced at her watch. "Why don't I meet you at the parsonage in an hour." From the frown on Blake's face when she suggested that, she knew he must have had other plans for them.

"No, I don't want to do this there," Gary complained. "Dad will have his nose in it. And your apartment's hot as blazes without the air. I could just meet you at the ice cream parlor."

"Jenna," Blake interrupted.

"Hold on a minute, Gary." She said to Blake, "It's my brother. I'm supposed to help him toss around ideas for a video tonight and I forgot all about it. He has to get this assignment moving."

"Tell him to come here. That will give us a little more time to talk."

"Oh, I can't—"

"Sure, you can. I have plenty of work to do in my office. After you two are finished, then maybe we can finish our discussion."

At first Jenna was ready to dismiss the idea, but then she thought about Gary, who was young but a good judge of character. She'd like his opinion of Blake.

Returning to the phone, she made the suggestion to her brother. "I'm at the old Van Heusen house."

"That mausoleum?"

She smiled. "If you want to put it that way."

"I've always wanted to see inside that place. Sure, sounds cool."

After Jenna slipped her phone back in her purse, she

said to Blake, "Gary's always been curious about this house. We used to take walks out here and circle the grounds."

"How old did you say your brother was?"

"He's seventeen, going on thirty."

Blake smiled and then sobered. "Are you going to tell him why you're here?"

"Yes. I don't keep secrets from Gary...unless you'd prefer I keep this quiet."

"It makes no difference to me. Word will get out. It always does."

With Blake Winston involved, she supposed that was true. Soon she'd have to tell her father she was carrying Blake's child.

Jenna was quiet after that, with both of them stealing glances at the other trying to figure out where they stood and what was going to come next. As if Blake had taken her comment seriously about getting to know him, he avoided discussion about custody and led her into small talk. Jenna found herself telling Blake about her second-grade classes and some of their escapades the previous year. She found satisfaction when he smiled and laughed, and she guessed he was a man who was too serious much of the time. Laughing had been second nature to B.J., and a smile had never been far from his face.

Her fork with its ball of cantaloupe stopped midway to her mouth. She shouldn't be comparing the two men. Why was she?

"Something wrong?" Blake asked.

She set down her fork with the uneaten cantaloupe. "No, I'm just getting full."

He cocked his head and his gray eyes were concerned. "You haven't eaten very much, especially since you're doing it for two."

Taking a deep breath, she decided to be honest. "The truth is, Blake, my stomach's been in knots since the clinic called me. You can't expect me to sit here and enjoy a meal with you while I'm worried about losing a child that I thought would be all mine."

His mouth tightened and his demeanor became defensive. "You're not going to lose this baby, Jenna. You're just going to have to share him or her."

"You can't share a child as if it's a piece of furniture that you can use in one house some of the time and in another house another part of the time. Children are resilient, Blake, but they're delicate, too. I've seen over and over again what happens when parents divorce and children are shuttled from one home to another when they don't understand where they belong. I don't want that for my baby."

Blake was disconcerted at her outburst, as if he hadn't thought about any of that.

Jenna was wondering if she should have said so much when Marilyn came to the doorway of the porch. "Mr. Gary Seabring, sir."

In spite of the situation, Jenna almost smiled at the expression on Gary's face at being introduced that way.

Gary was tall and lanky, his hair darker than Jenna's, his eyes more golden brown than the chocolate of hers. He moved into the room with the youthful energy he never tried to contain. "This is some place," he said with genuine admiration.

Standing, Blake extended his hand. "Glad you like it. I'm Blake Winston."

With a grin, Gary shook Blake's hand. He carried a notebook under his arm. "Thanks for letting me meet

Jenna here. Her apartment's hot as blazes and the ice cream parlor's too noisy.''

Blake turned to Jenna. "Would you like to work out here or in the parlor?''

With night descending, the air was cooler and Jenna liked the outside feel of the porch. "This is fine.''

Blake nodded to the table. "I'll tell Marilyn to leave the fruit, cheese and breads. Gary might want to snack while he works.''

"Thanks a lot," Gary said with enthusiasm. "Shirley made tuna casserole for supper." He screwed up his nose. "Not one of my favorites.''

"Did Dad try to dissuade you again from making the video?''

"You know he did. But I ignored him. I didn't go back home after I called you so he probably thinks we're at your place.''

"Jenna told me you're making a video. Is this just a school project or a real interest?'' Blake asked.

Jenna saw Gary's whole face light up as he answered, "It's my future. I want to be a filmmaker. I'm hoping to get into USC. One more year and I can really go at it.''

Gary moved toward Jenna and put his notebook on the table. "Your garage doors were open when I came up the drive. Was that a seventies Mustang I saw in there?''

"You've got a good eye. Actually, it's a '69. Would you like to see it before you get started?''

"Would I? You bet.''

"Gary, you really shouldn't get home too late—''

"You're acting like a mom again, sis. It's summer. I've got till midnight.''

"Why don't you come with us, Jenna?'' Blake invited. "The rose garden is spectacular right now and I promise I won't keep Gary from his work for too long."

A walk in the rose garden did sound lovely. Agreeing to the tour, she and Gary followed Blake through the kitchen and out the back door.

Jenna had hardly taken a turn around the magnificent gardens alive with not only roses, but hibiscus, bougainvillea and impatiens, when Blake and Gary returned. Apparently Blake *was* conscious of the time. As they approached her, they bandied about car terms she didn't understand. It was obvious Gary enjoyed being with Blake.

After Blake said he was going to his office down the hall, he left Gary and Jenna on the porch.

Gary turned to her. "Neat guy. What's going on with you two? Are you dating him?"

"No! It's not like that. It's because of the baby." And then Jenna explained to her brother about the meeting at the clinic, spending the afternoon on Blake's boat and his invitation to dinner tonight.

"Holy tamales," Gary drawled when she was done. "What are you going to do about all of it? He seems like a really cool guy. And you've got to realize any kid of his, if you look at the bottom line, wouldn't have to worry about scholarships or grants, would always have the very best of everything."

Jenna paced the porch. "How important is that, Gary? I've always thought that love and time and attention are more valuable than money."

"You're right, I guess, but the money's nice to have."

"We've never wanted for anything," she said, staring at him steadily. "Working for what you want teaches you to appreciate it more."

Her brother shrugged. "Do you remember that summer Dad had to use the rest of his savings for our new car? You saw how worried he was over the next year that something would happen he couldn't cover. And look at you and B.J. All those hospital bills the insurance isn't paying. Wouldn't it be nice to know the money's there if you need it?"

"You're talking about security," she said softly.

"Not only security. I've never been farther south than San Diego, or farther north than Redding. A kid of Blake Winston's could see the world. That counts when there's so much to see, don't you think?"

Ever since that first meeting at the clinic, she'd been mulling over all of this.

"What if you take Blake to court and you lose?" Gary asked.

"I've asked myself that same question a million times. Half a loaf is definitely better than none. But this is my child we're talking about, Gary." Then she thought about what Shannon had said—joint custody doesn't have to mean half and half. Just how much was Blake willing to bend? She needed to find that out before she made her final decision.

Smiling at Gary, she motioned to the chairs at the table. "Come on. Let's work on that project of yours. It'll give me a break from thinking about all of this."

It was almost 10:00 p.m. when Jenna and Gary finished batting about ideas, and he had pages of notes. She'd hardly had to say anything, really. He'd simply used her as a sounding board to expand on the concepts he already wanted to present.

Her brother glanced at his watch. "I'm going to

scoot out without saying goodbye to Blake. I'm meeting Darby at her place to listen to some new CDs.''

''You've been spending a lot of time with her.''

''I like her,'' he said with a grin. ''And she's cool with the fact that Dad's a minister. That's really a wet blanket on my dating pool.''

Jenna laughed in spite of herself. ''Your dating pool's going to expand once you get to college, and it probably won't matter at all.''

''I have a feeling it will *always* matter,'' Gary said somberly. Gathering up his things, he went over to the porch door. ''Are you going to be all right? I mean being here alone and all?''

''I'll be fine. Blake's not going to twist my arm or make me sign anything I don't want to sign. We both know where we stand, and it's a matter of dealing with that. I have to tell Dad soon, but I want to make some sort of decision first.''

Her brother nodded as if he understood. ''I'll see you tomorrow.'' Before he let himself out the door, he called over his shoulder, ''Tell Blake I'll be glad to take a ride in that car anytime he wants.''

As Jenna took a deep breath and walked down the hall, she went over the proposition she was about to make to Blake. It seemed reasonable to her, but she didn't know if it would seem that way to him. There was only one way to find out.

The door to his office was open. A pool of yellow light shone from the stained-glass lamp on his desk onto the papers in front of him. There was a computer and printer to one side of the L-shaped desk, but neither was turned on.

She rapped lightly on the door and stepped into the richly furnished mahogany and hunter-green office.

"Is his project all sewn up?" Blake asked with a smile.

"He already knew what he wanted to do," she said, returning his smile. "He just wanted confirmation his ideas were good ones."

"He seems like a nice kid. Intelligent, too. Is he really serious about filmmaking?"

"He's been shooting film since he was ten."

Blake nodded, pushed his chair back and stood. "Would you like a glass of milk or something?"

"No. I'd like to talk to you. I'd like to suggest…an arrangement."

"What kind of arrangement?"

She moved closer to him. "Joint custody doesn't have to be exactly joint custody, half with me, half with you. As a child grows up, I would think his or her needs would change and sometimes more time with Dad would be better and other times more time with Mom would be better."

"So what are you suggesting?"

Taking a deep breath, she plunged in. "Well…I think a newborn needs to stay physically close to its mom—as I said, I'm was going to breast-feed. Besides that, you probably work long hours. I'd like to have the baby with me for the first three months. You could visit any time you want, and I'd be glad to bring the child to you. As you become more comfortable with a newborn, maybe then you could take care of him or her on weekends. We'd discuss the arrangement every few months and do whatever was best for our baby."

"And what if you and I don't agree on what's best?" he asked in a low voice.

"I guess at that point we'd have to let our lawyers work it out."

The silence in the den was heavy as Blake leaned against the desk, sitting on its edge, studying her. She felt as if he was seeing into her much too deeply.

"What you're suggesting is that I'd basically be a weekend father." He didn't seem to like the idea at all. After a pensive pause, he asked, "Are you going back to teaching after the baby's born?"

"I have about two months of sick days, but after that, yes, I'll have to."

"And what were you going to do with our child?"

"Find good day care."

He let the silence billow over them again. Finally, he straightened, towering six inches above her. "I have a better idea. If you marry me, I'll be a full-time father and you'll be a full-time mother. Don't you think that's a better solution?"

Chapter Five

"Marry you?" Jenna was aghast.

Blake had known this decision he'd made—one he'd thought about carefully and that had seemed so clear to him—would be a shock to Jenna. "Yes, marry me. It's the best solution for both of us."

Taking a step back, she insisted vehemently, "I don't *know* you."

"We could remedy that. We've already made a good start."

"Hardly."

He almost smiled at her tone, but the subject was too serious. Taking her hand in his, he let his thumb skim the top of it. He could feel her slight quiver and experienced his own start of desire at that simple touch. There was chemistry between them as well as a child, whether she'd admit it or not. Their discussion at dinner had made him think long and hard about all of it.

"Would marriage be so terrible?" he asked in a voice he didn't even recognize, because it was filled with tenderness and protectiveness he'd never felt for a woman in his adult life.

"Blake, you can't be serious. It could lead to disaster. Unless— Are you talking about a marriage on paper only or a real one?"

"I've considered both. I don't know what you mean by a real marriage, but I'm proposing a partnership. We'd live together, eventually sleep together. We'd both have constant and complete access to our child." It was a very practical solution as far as he was concerned.

"Eventually sleep together?"

The look in her eyes was part fear, part panic, with a spark of interest thrown in. If he trod very carefully here, he might get what he wanted. He didn't believe the chemistry was just on his side, but he realized for Jenna it was complicated.

Turning her hand over, he brought it to his lips and kissed her upturned palm. A small gasp escaped her as he touched her skin with his tongue.

Her cheeks flushed with color, and he never took his eyes from her. "There's attraction between us, Jenna, whether you want to admit it or not. I know this is difficult for you. Your husband hasn't been gone that long and—"

"I loved B.J.," she said fervently.

"I believe you did…that you do." Blake couldn't understand his own disappointed response to that fact. It wasn't as if he believed in love. It wasn't as if he believed in marriage as a joining of souls, a level of commitment that could match no other. He'd never seen it. On some level he knew his father's love for his mother had destroyed his dad. After his mom died, his father had missed her so desperately that he'd wanted to join her. For years he'd dealt with that idea by withdrawing into a liquor induced haze.

Blake never wanted to love anyone that much. When he'd mistakenly thought he'd found love with Danielle, she'd shown him love meant betrayal as well as heartache. Although she'd said she loved him, when it came time to prove it she'd given in to her father's bribe instead of standing beside Blake and admitting her feelings for him. Then again, over the years Blake had realized her feelings hadn't been as strong as her desire to do her father's bidding or her need for financial advantages Blake couldn't yet give her.

All that only strengthened his resolve. "No matter how much you want to believe otherwise, this child *isn't* B.J.'s. It's mine, and I'm not going to let you pretend differently. It will have *my* DNA, not his."

He wasn't used to putting how he felt into words, but now he tried. "I want to be a full-time father. I want to live under the same roof—see my child eat that sticky cereal in the mornings, check on him in his crib late at night. I want to see his first smile, watch the first tooth break through, see his first step. And I know you do, too. If you marry me, you'd have no need for day care. You could stay home and take care of this baby. You'd have access day and night to rock, to sing, to feed, to carry this baby. Isn't that what you want, Jenna?"

He saw her mulling it over and knew he was making a good case. At the outset it had sounded crazy, but the more they examined the intricate details of this partnership, the more it made sense.

Pulling her hand away from his, she went over to

the window and looked out at the floodlit garden. "You'd be tying yourself up," she said practically. "You'd be tied to me and this child." Swinging around to face him again, she asked, "Isn't there a woman you want to share all this with you? I don't deserve it. I don't have a right to it. I don't belong here."

He suspected those were arguments she was making for herself so she could reject the whole premise. "You're carrying my child. You belong here."

She shook her head. "You know what I mean. Isn't there someone you care about? Someone you want to spend the rest of your life with?"

Fleetingly, he considered what Nolan Constantine had told him about Danielle Howard being back in town. But that was water over the dam. After Danielle, he hadn't let himself get close to *any* woman, and he doubted he'd let himself get close to Jenna, either. She had to understand that.

"I don't believe in fairy tales, Jenna. I can believe in a decision two people make and the commitment they adhere to. There's no one special I care about. There hasn't been for almost twenty years. I'm not sentimental. I don't believe in Cupid. The only bond that can last is one based on common goals. We have a common goal—the successful raising of our child."

She still looked troubled, and he wasn't surprised by what she asked next. "You said you'd eventually want to…sleep together. How soon?"

Not sure about pregnancy and when sex was appropriate and when it wasn't, he knew this could be a big stumbling block for Jenna.

"We could wait until after the baby's born. That would give us time to get to know each other and get used to the idea of us being together and having the baby.''

''You have everything worked out,'' she said, as if it wasn't a compliment.

''I've turned this inside out and upside down. I've spoken to my lawyer. I searched case law myself. I've considered everything you've said and everything I want. I think you're the kind of woman who won't want to be separated from her baby for a minute. You'll find it difficult to say goodbye when he or she goes to kindergarten for the first day, and when our son or daughter leaves for college, you'll cry your eyes out.''

Judging from the way she ducked her head and the way her eyelashes fluttered down, he knew he was right. She didn't want him to see *how* right.

He tipped her chin up with his forefinger. ''I think you'll make a wonderful mother, and I want to be the best dad this child could ever have.''

They were standing close now. Her belly was almost touching his belt buckle. She smelled so sweet, looked so damn pretty, created a need inside of him that was going to be hard to deny for three months. Still, he knew he couldn't push her because he might make her run scared. ''I know you need to think about this, and we need to spend time together. I have tickets for the theater tomorrow night. Will you go with me?''

''I can't,'' she replied quickly. ''I have a parenting-childbirth class. It's the first one, and I don't want to miss it.''

''Do you need a coach?'' He didn't know *much* about it, but he did know women in labor needed someone to help with breathing.

''I asked Shannon.''

''Do you think she'd mind if you let me be your

coach? Or maybe we could do it together. More than anything, I want to see this child brought into the world.'' When he saw the hesitation in Jenna's eyes, he wanted to insist again that he was the father, that he had rights. But with Jenna that might not work. He had to go about this diplomatically. If he didn't, he'd be talking to Rafe Pierson instead of to the mother of his baby.

''Let me think about all this until tomorrow. All right?'' Jenna asked him, her eyes large and troubled.

It wasn't all right. He wanted her answer now…to everything. But he knew patience. It was a quality he needed most in security work.

''Tomorrow, it is.'' Deciding to give her some leeway, he added, ''About the coaching question, anyway. The rest…you think about it until you settle it in your head.''

When Jenna gave him a grateful smile, he knew he'd said the right thing. He had to keep saying the right thing until he convinced her to marry him. After that…they'd work everything out one day at a time.

Jenna slipped into Shirley's desk chair on Thursday morning, her mind swirling with all the decisions she had to make. She'd called Shannon last night to discuss whether or not Blake should be her coach. In a kind way, Shannon had said she'd been looking forward to the experience but understood if Jenna wanted the father there. She could be on call in case Blake couldn't make it. She knew all the steps of natural childbirth since she'd been through it herself.

Shannon's understanding helped, and Jenna thought about telling her friend about Blake's marriage proposal. Yet something kept her from doing that.

Before she'd left her apartment for the parsonage, she'd phoned Blake and told him he could be her coach. When she'd suggested Shannon could be backup, he'd agreed in case he was called out of town. But he would try to be available for every session and definitely be present at the birth.

Jenna knew life didn't always go as planned.

She'd just switched on the computer and was going to start printing the weekly Sunday church bulletin when her father stopped in the office. He stood watching her for a few moments. "You were quiet at breakfast this morning."

"I guess I'm just a little tired. I didn't sleep well last night."

"That grandchild of mine keeping you awake?"

It wasn't the baby's kicking that had kept her tossing and turning, but rather Blake's marriage proposal. "It was just a restless night."

"I understand you had dinner at Blake Winston's last night."

Her astonishment must have shown.

"I knew you and Gary were meeting to work on his project and your air-conditioning was out. I asked him where you met. He told me."

"What else did he tell you?" she asked cautiously, sure Gary wouldn't give away more than he had to. He would have told the truth, but hopefully the barest of it.

"Is there something more to tell?" her father asked probingly.

Usually she answered her father's questions patiently, but this morning they annoyed her. "What do you want to know, Dad?"

He looked disconcerted by her tone. "I want to

know if you're seeing the man. It hasn't been that long, Jenna—''

"I know very well how long it's been since B.J. died. I still get up every morning and go to bed every night missing him." Though what bothered her now was the fact Blake appeared in her dreams rather than B.J.

"Have you seen the Wintons lately?"

Charlene and Bill Winton wanted her to drop in often so they could stay connected to their grandchild. But now she'd have to tell them this baby *wasn't* their grandchild. "I had dinner with them last week."

"They're good people. If they hear you're seeing somebody so soon, it might upset them."

More than her seeing Blake was going to upset them. "All my life I've tried to please other people. Now I have to do what's best for me."

Her father didn't look happy with that comment. "That means seeing Blake Winston? I don't understand why the man would want to have anything to do with you." He must have realized how that sounded. "I mean, you're pregnant! His picture's always in the paper with those career types."

It was the perfect opening to tell him exactly what was going on, but she couldn't make herself do that. She didn't want to be swayed by what *he* thought she should do. Talking with her father wasn't like talking to Shannon, working through a problem, or making the best decision on her own. Talking to her father was always like talking to an all-knowing figure who had the right answer and wouldn't tolerate the wrong one.

"Blake and I are becoming friends."

Her father cocked an eyebrow at that. "Gary told me about the Mustang and how Winston's fixed up the

Van Heusen place. Men like that don't know where their money can do the most good. Men like that are selfish, Jenna. They think they can own the world and everyone in it.''

"You don't know Blake, Dad."

"Are you telling me he's not that way?"

Jenna followed her instincts about people. B.J. had been a simple man—what you saw was what you got. He'd been outgoing and plain speaking and she'd loved that about him. Blake, on the other hand, seemed to have developed a few sharp edges to guard himself. He shared little and expected a lot. From small things he'd said, she'd deduced his childhood hadn't been an easy one. Yet she didn't know why. There were so many levels to the man, and she'd only seen a few of them. Underneath all of it, she sensed a good heart that he kept locked up tight except where this baby was concerned.

"I only met Blake recently. I like him, and Gary does, too."

"Your brother is too easily impressed by trappings that shouldn't matter."

Sometimes she didn't think her father knew her brother at all. "Gary's a good judge of character whether you believe that or not." Wanting this conversation to end before she said something she shouldn't, she flipped on the printer, took out the paper tray and loaded it with paper.

"Watch your step, Jenna," her father warned her.

She didn't know if he was talking about her attitude with him or her friendship with Blake. Knowing her father needed to have the last word, she didn't respond but went about the task of printing out the weekly bulletin.

Her father's voice was brisk when he said, "I have some sick calls to make. I'll be back around one."

"There are leftovers from last night. I'll make a salad to go with them for you. Will you and Gary be okay for supper? I have a parenting class."

"We'll be fine. I'll take Gary to that submarine sandwich shop he likes so much. You don't have to worry about meals for the weekend. Shirley left plenty of casseroles."

She was relieved because she had no idea what her weekend was going to bring. It all depended on what decision she made.

When Blake and Jenna arrived at the hospital where the parenting course was being given, they exchanged a look before stepping into the classroom. Blake had had trouble keeping his mind on driving on the way over. Jenna was dressed in denim slacks and a white-and-red checked overblouse tonight. All he could think about was having her as a wife. He'd never particularly taken notice of pregnant women before, but there was something about Jenna, some quality that created a yearning in his chest. Maybe it had just been too long since he'd taken a woman to bed. Yet why did he feel this way about a pregnant one?

Because she's carrying your child.

"Are you ready for this?" he asked with a smile.

"As ready as I can be."

He thought she sounded anxious.

When they stepped into the room, there were three other couples milling around. The woman who was teaching the class invited them inside, offering them punch and cookies, which were laid out on a long table. She instructed, "Write your names on name tags and familiarize yourselves with the products we have sitting around. There are diapers and baby food and car seats. It will give you an idea of the decisions you'll have to make. In about five minutes I'll introduce everyone, and we'll get started.''

After Jenna and Blake wrote their first names on tags and attached them to their shirts, they wandered over to the table where another couple were standing. A lanky man with blond hair and wire-rimmed glasses was saying to his wife, ''Look at the price on those diapers...the baby food. And we were worried about a college education!''

Blake saw the frown that crossed Jenna's face, and he knew she was probably worrying about the economics of having a child. If she married him, she wouldn't have to worry about that. He caught sight of a doll in the car seat, and the reality of having a baby gripped him. He'd never even held an infant. How would he know what to do? How would he know when to pick up the child and when not to? When to feed it and when not to? Jenna was examining a can of formula and he realized he needed her mothering skills as much as she needed to be economically secure.

After she lifted and examined a slanted bottle that was designed to prevent gas, she murmured, ''So many decisions to make.''

''And how do you know if you're making the right one?''

She gave him a small smile. ''This is never going to end, is it? Once we have a baby, it will be decisions and uncertainty and responsibility for the rest of our lives.''

He was pleased at the words she'd used—once *we* have a baby. ''I've never thought about it that way before, but you're right. It's an exciting prospect, though, isn't it?''

''I think the excitement is what helped me not panic since I found out I was pregnant. Every day will be new and different and I'll learn something about my child.''

This time he reminded her, ''*Our* child.''

When their eyes locked, the excitement he felt encompassed more than a new baby. His work sometimes made his adrenaline rush. Taking the Mustang out on a straightaway could, too. But when he looked into Jenna's eyes, he could feel the crackle of chemistry between them that was stronger than anything he'd ever felt before. When he saw her take a deep breath, clutch her purse tighter and turn away, he was sure she felt it, too.

The first part of the class was the basics—what natural childbirth was and wasn't, how a coach could help, the reminder that breathing was everything. Before Blake knew it, they were on the floor on mats and he was sitting behind Jenna holding her up as she practiced different types of breathing techniques. She was warm under his hands, her skin was smooth, her scent flowery. He realized keeping his desire out of this mix was going to be damn difficult. More than once she started when he touched her, more than once her eyes skidded away from his, and more than once he got the feeling she hadn't made up her mind yet about his proposal.

At break time, they nibbled cookies and drank punch while they spoke with the other couples. He thought Jenna looked pale as they started down the corridor to take a tour of the hospital's nursery and birthing rooms.

In the maternity wing, Blake could see sweat beading on Jenna's brow. "Are you all right?"

"I don't think those cookies agreed with me. I'm feeling queasy. I think I'd better—"

She darted away from him, and he realized she'd headed for a bathroom they'd passed. She'd gotten ahead of him and when he tried to turn the knob on the door, it was locked. He rapped sharply. "Jenna! Jenna, let me in."

Her mumbled voice came through the door. "I'm okay. Just give me a few minutes."

"Jenna, open the door," he demanded. He knew she probably didn't want him seeing her being sick, but if she needed medical help...

The door didn't open for another few seconds and then the lock clicked.

Blake thrust down the lever and pushed the door open. Jenna was standing at the sink with the water running. She was ashen and her pallor worried him.

Splashing water on her face, she murmured, "I'll be fine."

"Does this happen often?" he asked gruffly.

"When I get too hot, tired or eat something I shouldn't. I should have known better than to try those spice cookies."

He almost smiled at the resignation in her voice. "Do you want to stay?"

She shook her head. "The tour of the hospital isn't as important as the rest of the class, and that's all they're going to do for the rest of tonight. I think you'd better take me home."

Just one look at Jenna's face convinced Blake she was right about that. He was disappointed they wouldn't be spending the rest of the evening together.

He'd envisioned going somewhere afterward, buying her a glass of milk, or whatever else pregnant women drank. But there would be other nights.

Fifteen minutes later as they walked up the steps to her apartment, he felt as if she was taking them slowly.

"Are you sure these steps are good for you?"

She glanced at him and gave him a wan smile. "Exercise is an important part of staying fit while I'm pregnant. I haven't had any trouble with the steps. I'm just a bit tired."

"Did you rest today?"

"I didn't get a chance. Dad's secretary's gone until Tuesday, and I'm filling in for her."

Before Blake could say what was on his mind, Jenna insisted, "Some women work until the day before they give birth, so don't tell me handling a few secretarial skills is too taxing."

"You've got to take care of yourself," he muttered.

"I am." At the top of the steps, she extracted her key from her purse.

A few minutes later when she opened her door and they stepped inside, Blake knew Jenna couldn't stay here tonight. "Your air-conditioning's still not fixed?"

"Not yet. Any day now."

"You're not sleeping, are you?" he asked perceptively.

"The temperature cools off by morning."

He shook his head. "Jenna, it's at least ninety-five degrees in here. You can't stay here tonight." In spite of the heat, she was still looking pale.

She put her hand to her forehead and rubbed her brow wearily. "No, I guess I can't. I'll have to go to the parsonage."

Hearing the uncertain note in her voice, he picked up on it. "You don't sound as if you want to do that."

"I don't," she said with a small laugh. "But it's better than paying a motel bill."

"You still haven't told your father about the baby."

"No. I have decisions to make first." Her gaze met his, and they both knew what the biggest of those would be.

"Come home with me," he suggested impulsively.

"What?"

"No one has to know." He added, "No one except Marilyn. My house is air-conditioned. The guest room always has fresh sheets. You could go to bed early and sleep as late as you want. Marilyn will bring you breakfast in bed if you'd like."

She looked tempted. "That sounds too good to be true."

"It's not," he said as casually as he could. "You'd have a completely stress-free environment. It would be like being on a vacation."

"I don't know, Blake." Their eyes met again. "And as far as it being stress-free..."

He held up his hands in a surrender mode. "I promise I won't exert any pressure on you to give me an answer about my marriage proposal. This will be rest and relaxation for as long as you need it."

"Till morning," she finally agreed. "I can't stay with you, Blake, but I could use a good night's sleep and some relief from the heat."

"Then it's decided." Before she could change her mind, he added, "Just pack up a few things and we'll be out of here."

Less than an hour later, Blake was showing Jenna to a guest room on the second floor of his house. She didn't even feel as if she were climbing the steps on the plush carpeting, and she wondered if she was making the biggest mistake of her life. While she'd packed, Blake had called ahead and Marilyn had met them at the door. She'd offered to take Jenna's bag, but Blake had said he'd take care of it. But he did ask the housekeeper to bring Jenna a tall glass of water, a glass of milk, saltines and anything else that was light enough for her to enjoy.

Never in her life having been so pampered, Jenna was already beginning to feel better in the cool interior.

Blake led her down a hall and motioned to the far end. "My suite's down there."

Taking her inside a room that was decorated in yellow and lavender flowers, she saw him gesture to the buzzer on the wall beside the bed. "If you need anything, that will bring Marilyn. Or—" he paused "—you can always come and get me." He laid her overnight case on a lavender velvet chair.

"I'm sure I'll be fine."

Crossing to her, he studied her carefully. "You look better. You really had me scared. You were gray around the gills."

"It's a good thing you didn't see me the first two months of my pregnancy, then. I was sick every morning and every night."

"You shouldn't have been working."

Men! Sometimes they didn't have a clue. "Thank goodness I *was* working. Those little kids gave me the energy I lacked. Teaching kept me on my feet, and I ate because I knew I had to. It's all just part of the process and it passed."

"Except for tonight."

"That was the cookies."

"Or maybe the stress of everything that's going on."

She couldn't deny that. Between the news about the baby being Blake's child, the heat in her apartment and trying to make the best decisions for her child...*their* child, who wouldn't be stressed? "I'm feeling much better. Really I am. I can't wait to get a shower, brush my teeth and actually get a good night's sleep."

There was a knock on the door and Marilyn stood there with a tray.

"You make yourself comfortable," Blake said. "I have a few calls to make, then I'll be back to make sure you're settled in for the night."

Before she could protest that wasn't necessary, Blake was out the door and Marilyn was setting the tray in the small sitting area. Jenna thanked her, then headed for the bathroom.

She had brushed her teeth at her apartment but did it again now, taking in the green feminine ambience of the bathroom. The violet towels were luxurious and the leaf-green bath mat caressed her toes. As she showered, she used an imported soap that made her skin feel silky. Drying her hair with a small white dryer on the vanity, she smiled at herself in the mirror, feeling not only much better, but more feminine than she'd felt in a long time. After she'd brushed her hair into soft waves around her face, she slipped on the white cotton night-gown and robe she'd brought from her apartment. It was edged in pink embroidered roses. She'd found the ensemble at the thrift shop. The tags had still been attached as if no one had ever worn it. Besides the debt she owed, she'd been trying to save money for the extras she'd need.

She was sipping water and eating a few saltines

when there was a knock on her door. She knew it would be Blake and her heart raced.

When she opened the door, he had a few magazines in his hand. "I didn't know if you read these or not. I bought them yesterday."

Taking them from him, she saw *Parents*, *Baby Talk* and *The American Family*. "Have *you* read them?" she asked, taking them into the room and placing them on the bed.

He followed her. "Yes. I never knew raising a child could be so complicated. One of them lists everything you need before the baby's born."

"I'll make sure I look at it."

Taking her by the shoulders, he insisted, "Jenna, you can stay here as long as you want."

"Only tonight, Blake."

"What if your air-conditioning isn't fixed?"

"Then I'll go to the parsonage. I have to tell Dad everything that's happening sometime."

Blake's very gray eyes were filled with the question he wanted an answer to, but he'd promised not to push her and he didn't voice it again.

Suddenly she was very aware that she was in her nightgown and robe in a bedroom with a man who was practically a stranger. Marilyn was far away downstairs. Jenna knew she shouldn't be this trusting, she knew she shouldn't be enjoying the feel of Blake's hands on her shoulders, she knew the images flitting through her mind didn't belong there.

"I would never do anything you wouldn't want me to do, Jenna."

Sometimes he seemed to read her mind, and she wondered if he could do that with everyone or just with her.

Why with her?

Why, indeed. She couldn't move her eyes from his…she couldn't move, period. Something about him held her still, held her captive, filled her with yearnings she hadn't experienced since way before B.J. died.

When Blake bent his head, she didn't move away. As his lips hovered over hers, she lifted her chin slightly. Then he was kissing her in a way she'd never been kissed—thoroughly, masterfully, sweepingly. His arms came around her and she felt safe enough to lift her hands to his shoulders, to lean into his body, to prolong the kiss. His tongue swept her mouth, and she became hot, felt her body blossom, and gave herself up to passion that had never overwhelmed her like this before.

Blake was the one to break away, and when he did, he stared down at her with so many questions, she couldn't begin to answer them.

Mortified, she backed away. "I shouldn't have done that."

"Jenna…"

"I shouldn't have. I'm pregnant. B.J.'s still…I mean…it must have been hormones."

At that his brows quirked up. "I'd say that was an understatement."

Thoroughly flustered now, she saw her overnight case on the chair and went toward it. "I shouldn't stay. I should go back to my apartment, go to the parsonage. I could even go to Shannon and Rafe's—"

He cut her off by taking her by the shoulders. "Stop it, Jenna. Don't get yourself into a tizzy about this. It was only a kiss."

Only a kiss. Only a kiss that had shaken her life.

Only a kiss that made her wonder what her values were, what her love for B.J. had been, what it still was.

"You don't have to leave. I will." He released her shoulders but looked at her sternly. "And don't think you're going to sneak out before breakfast. I want to make sure you had a good night's sleep and a decent meal before you go."

"I should have driven myself here. I wasn't thinking. I can call Gary in the morning and he can pick me up."

"I'll take you wherever you have to go."

"You can just take me back to my apartment. I told Dad I'd make him and Gary lunch and then work through the afternoon."

"All right," he agreed, apparently seeing her determination. He crossed to the door. "Remember, if you need anything, I'm down the hall."

When Blake left, he closed the door behind him.

Jenna wasn't sure what she needed from this handsome, confident, complex man. Looking at the magazines on the bed, tears came to her eyes. B.J. never would have gone out and bought the magazines. He'd had two brothers and a sister and was used to being around kids. He would have said, "Jenna, there's nothing we can't learn by just taking care of them."

But Blake was a different kind of man, and this was *his* child.

Maybe telling her father about the baby wasn't such a bad idea, after all. She certainly needed guidance from someone.

Chapter Six

*B*eep, *beep, beep.*

Jenna heard the ring of her cell phone and sat up in bed. She suddenly realized she wasn't in her own bed but at Blake's house in his guest room. Then she remembered the kiss—

Beep, beep, beep.

Scrambling out of bed, she fished her phone out of her purse on the dresser. "Hello?" she answered breathlessly.

"Where are you?" Gary asked with a bit of worry and exasperation.

It seemed everyone wanted to keep tabs on her. "You wouldn't believe me if I told you."

"Try me. I've been calling your apartment since seven-thirty. I thought maybe you were in the shower or something. But when you still didn't answer after an hour…"

She checked the bedside clock and saw that it was eight-thirty. "I'm at Blake's."

She heard his low whistle. "I hope I'm not interrupting anything."

"It's not like that. He took me to my first parenting class and I didn't feel well. When we went back to my apartment, it was so hot I knew I wouldn't get any sleep if I stayed there. I'm in one of his guest rooms. You can't tell Dad."

"Of course I won't tell Dad. You know me better than that. I don't have to go to work till noon and I thought I could run a few scenes by you."

The burden of keeping the clinic's mistake from her father was becoming too great a one. She needed to tell him what was going on. She was sure he would have plenty of advice. He always did. "Instead of going back to my apartment, I'll come over to the parsonage this morning. I have to talk to Dad and tell him what's going on. After that, we can work on anything you want."

"Sounds good. Want me to come pick you up?"

"I'll call you if I need you."

Jenna didn't know what Blake had in mind for this morning, if anything. She'd better find out about that first.

When she went downstairs, Marilyn met her in the hall with a wide smile. "Mr. Blake told me not to get you up, to let you sleep. He's in his office working. What would you like for breakfast?"

"Just toast is fine."

Marilyn looked over Jenna. "I think I'll whip up some scrambled eggs with that. A little protein wouldn't hurt in your condition. I'm sure Mr. Blake will think the same thing."

"Has he eaten breakfast yet?"

"Oh, he's always up before the sun. I fed him around six-thirty. It'll take me about ten minutes to get everything ready. The morning paper's out on the porch if you're interested."

"I think I'll tell Blake I'm up."

After Marilyn nodded and bustled toward the kitchen, Jenna went down the hall and stopped when she glimpsed Blake through the open door. He was sitting at his desk, typing on the computer keyboard.

When she knocked softly, he turned away from the screen.

"Good morning," she said with a smile.

Immediately he pressed a key. After the screen went blank, he stood and came around the desk. His eyes passed over her in a quick appraisal that seemed to miss nothing—from her hair pulled into a barrette over her temple, to her turquoise knit top, to her pristine white shorts and sandals.

"You look rested," he said with satisfaction.

"I feel more rested than I have in a week. Thanks for offering a spare room."

"You can stay again tonight."

"No, that's not a good idea."

She could see he disagreed with her by the tightening of his jaw, but he didn't say anything.

"I want to go over to the parsonage this morning and tell Dad everything. Gary said he'd pick me up, so if you're not going out—"

"I'm going with you."

For a moment she was horrified. "That's not a good idea."

"This affects both our lives, Jenna. Your father has

to know I'm not going to go away simply because he doesn't want you to have anything to do with me.''

"He never said that."

"No, but I could see he thought it. I know he's not going to like the idea of me being the father of his grandchild, and you shouldn't have to take all the flak by yourself."

Would it be better to have Blake along or would that only make the situation worse? "I think I should do this alone."

"I'll tell you what. I'll drop you off and wait outside. You can talk to him alone for a while and when you finish, we can talk to him together."

"It's not as if we've decided what we're going to do yet." Knowing her father, she still didn't like this strategy.

Blake was adamant. "I want to make sure your father knows any decision we make is ours to make— yours and mine, not his."

All of this troubled her. "I feel as if you're taking over. I feel as if you think I don't have a strong-enough will to stand up to him."

"Do you?"

She was learning quickly to expect blunt honesty from Blake at all times, and she supposed that was best. "You have to trust me," she responded quietly.

"I don't trust anyone, Jenna."

She could see that was true, but she could also see that he hadn't *had* to trust anybody. "If we're both going to be parents to this baby, we have to trust each other."

This morning he was wearing a beige oxford shirt and black casual slacks. His shirt sleeves were rolled back, and as he came toward her now, she had a tummy-twirling feeling that had nothing to do with the baby. When he towered over her, she inhaled the scent of his cologne, could feel the force of his virility as if it were a shield around him.

Staying focused, she appealed to reason. "We especially have to trust each other if we raise this baby in separate households." Her heart sank at that thought. "I have to trust you to do what's best, and you have to trust me. We can't be second-guessing each other. That's the worst thing parents can do when they're raising a child."

A few silent moments ticked by, then with a wry expression, Blake asked, "You're a fighter in disguise, aren't you? You don't build walls I have to break down, but you hold up a mirror so I have to see more than my side."

She thought about that. "While I was growing up, Dad ruled with an iron hand. With him, a situation is black or white—there's no gray, and there's always a right answer. Openly defying him wouldn't have gotten me anywhere."

"You're a powerful woman, Jenna Winton," Blake said, as if he were seeing her in a new way.

"Me? I don't think so."

Slowly he raised his hand and gently brushed her hair behind her ear. His fingers lingered there. "Humble, too." He rimmed the shell of her ear with his thumb and she felt tingles everywhere inside of her. "And very kissable," he added, his voice lowering in timbre.

Though she wanted to feel his lips on hers again, though she was curious about everything he'd awakened inside of her, she felt so guilty about those feelings. B.J. still owned her heart and she didn't know if she wanted to change that. She didn't know if she was ready to let a man like Blake into her life. Yet she might not have any choice.

Placing her hands on his chest, she shook her head. "Not again, Blake. I'm not ready for that."

Although he looked disappointed, after a moment the neutral expression he wore often was back in place. "And I said I wouldn't rush you. I'll back off, Jenna. I'm a man of my word."

She believed he was. She also believed in some ways he was as implacable as her father. She didn't know if she was any more ready for their clash than she was for Blake's kiss. "You don't have to talk to my father today."

"Yes, I do. He has to know I won't give up rights to my child."

Suddenly she knew Blake wouldn't give up anything that he wanted badly, maybe because he'd had to give up too much along the way.

An hour later, Blake pulled up in front of the parsonage. "You're going to get hot in the car," Jenna said. "There's a swing in the backyard."

"I'll be fine. I have my briefcase and phone here. I can make a few calls. I have an event coming up in less than three weeks and everything has to be in order for it."

She really wasn't sure exactly what he did. "What kind of an event?"

"Senator Evanston is speaking in Sacramento. We're handling security. It will be tighter than usual."

She imagined that security was tighter than usual everywhere now. "What does that mean?"

"It means the men I selected for bodyguards are

particularly well trained. It means I'll have video cameras positioned to cover everyone all the time. There will be metal detectors at the door and no one will get through without being screened. I've done background checks on the five hundred people who've bought dinner tickets, and we'll ID them when they come in.''

"Is this mostly the kind of thing you do?''

"Not necessarily. My firm also makes sure companies' computer systems are as hacker-proof as possible, puts in alarm systems, does background investigations.''

"That's how you knew where to go to find out things about…me.''

"It's what I do, Jenna. It's second nature. Information is always power and a lot of people know that.''

When she still didn't make a move to get out of the car, he asked with a twitch of his lips, "Are you procrastinating?''

She shook her head. "Just shoring up my courage.'' She lifted the door handle and grabbed her overnight bag.

Not wanting to call attention to Blake's car out front, she went around the path to the back of the house and let herself in the kitchen door. After she talked to her father, she should visit B.J.'s parents and explain to them what had happened. Facing them with this bombshell wouldn't be any easier than explaining it to her dad.

The house was quiet except for the ticking of the clock on the wall. Hoping her father was in his office, she dropped her bag on a kitchen chair and headed that way. Before she could find him, he found her.

As he came through the door of the parlor he often

used for counseling sessions, his expression was stern. "What's that man doing outside?" he asked her.

The parlor faced the street and he would have seen Blake drive up. "He brought me over here to talk to you. There's something I need to tell you."

Dressed in a white, oxford-cloth shirt and black trousers, her father motioned to the parlor. He was a no-nonsense, let's-get-to-the-root-of-the-problem kind of counselor, and now she knew he wouldn't let her ease into this slowly. Sitting on one of the rust tweed wing chairs, she folded her hands in her lap, reminding herself to stay calm. "Why don't you sit down, Dad?"

"I'm fine," he said, leaning against the desk. "I want to know what's going on between you and Blake Winston."

She knew her father was concerned for her and he was brusque because of that. "I was called into the Emerson Clinic on Tuesday. They made a mistake when they did the insemination. The technician pulled the wrong vial. I'm carrying Blake Winston's child, not B.J.'s."

The words hung in the small parlor and seemed to boomerang off the pine-paneled walls.

When her father didn't speak, Jenna added, "Blake and I are trying to find a solution."

"There is no solution to this kind of situation," her father said with a shake of his head. "Didn't I tell you using unorthodox means to get pregnant would only cause trouble? It's not natural."

She wasn't going to get into *that* discussion again. "I know what you said. I understand how you feel. But saying 'I told you so' now really doesn't help. This baby I'm carrying is a reality, and Blake wants to be a part of his or her life as much as I do."

"What kind of solution can you come up with? Why aren't you just going to court and fighting for this child?" her father asked bluntly.

"Because I might lose." That was her absolute worst fear.

Charles shook his head and ran his hands through his hair. "I can't believe it's not B.J.'s. At least then we would have known everything there was to know about its father."

"Blake's a good man."

"How can you know that? Did you know him before all of this happened?"

"No, but I've spent some time with him the past few days."

"And you think you know him after a few days? A man like Blake Winston's going to show you exactly what he wants you to see. You're no match for someone as worldly as him. He might be manipulating you—"

At that moment, Blake pushed open the door to the parlor and stepped inside. His deep voice had an edge to it when he asked, "Are you all right, Jenna?"

From Blake's expression, Jenna could see that he was worried about her. He'd obviously come inside to help her deal with her father.

"She's fine, Winston. We don't need you involved in this discussion," her father said bluntly.

"That's exactly the point, Reverend Seabring. I think you do. To put it plainly, Jenna can't afford a court battle. I can. But Jenna is the mother of this child and I know that counts in front of a judge, too. Neither of us believe a court battle is best for us or for the baby. We're trying to work out something else. At the least, joint custody."

Jenna hoped Blake wasn't going to tell her father about the marriage proposal. She didn't want him to have a stroke on the spot. "Blake..." she warned.

"I know, Jenna."

"You know what?" Charles Seabring asked angrily.

"I know I intend to be a full-time father one way or another. I just want *you* to know that, Reverend Seabring. Don't think you're going to convince Jenna to cut me out of this baby's life."

The resounding silence in the room made Jenna cross to Blake and place a hand on his arm. "Can I talk to you for a minute outside?"

Blake glanced at her father and then back at her. "All right."

They stepped outside the small room, and Blake looked as if he wanted to slam the door on her father and everything he represented.

She looked up at him. "You've made your point, Blake. Now let me talk to my dad on my own."

"He's going to try to fill your head with—"

"I told you before, I make my own decisions. But he *is* this baby's grandfather and I want him in my child's life."

"Why?" Blake snapped. "He obviously makes judgments at the drop of a hat. He's going to hold a moral sword over your head instead of supporting you."

The reverend pushed the door open, his cheeks ruddy with agitation. "Don't you tell me about morality, Winston. I've seen your picture in the paper with a different woman every couple of months. Those articles make it very clear what kind of life you lead. That last interview you did was very revealing. You charter planes to fly to Reno to the casinos, you move in celebrity circles in L.A. Tell me how my daughter and her child are going to fit into all of that.''

''That's enough, Dad,'' Jenna said.

''I'm sure your father has a lot more to say,'' Blake remarked coolly. ''If he wants to say it, that's fine, but it won't change the bottom line. This child is mine and I have more say in its life than he does, no matter what kind of hold he has over you.''

''You've no right to talk to her like that,'' her father said. ''If you don't have the decency to realize a mother's bond to her child is sacred—''

''Stop!'' Jenna had put more force behind the word than she'd intended and both men's gazes snapped to her. ''Arguing won't do any good and both of you know that.'' Her eyes pleaded with Blake. ''Let me talk to my father alone.''

Blake's expression was hard, but it only took a few seconds for him to make up his mind. ''All right. Talk to him all day if you want. Just don't look to him for support. I don't think he knows how to give it.''

He held up his hand as if he knew she was going to defend her dad. ''I'm leaving. I'll call you.''

Then Blake walked down the hall away from them.

Jenna had the strangest urge to go with him, to defend him, to stand by his side. That was absolutely crazy, wasn't it? She didn't actually have feelings for Blake, did she? Not so soon. She couldn't.

But Blake's marriage proposal suddenly didn't seem as ridiculous as when he'd first suggested it.

The tenants in the apartment above Jenna's were having a party on Friday night. It was midnight, and she could hear the bass from the stereo pounding into her ceiling. Her apartment had held the heat from the day and even with the bedroom window wide open, the room was too warm to allow sleep. Switching on her bedside lamp, she plumped up the pillow against the headboard and leaned back against it, remembering the expression on Blake's face as he'd left her father's house.

Her discussion with her father after Blake left had been a short one. He disapproved of the way she'd conceived this child, he disapproved of her trying to settle this with Blake personally, he disapproved of Blake Winston on the basis of what he'd read in the paper and the rumors he'd heard around town. Then he'd told her something he thought would shock her— Blake's father had committed suicide. After she'd absorbed that, he'd gone on to say Blake had grown up in the poorer section of Fawn Grove, left the town as a teenager, and hadn't returned until three years ago. According to her father, he had too much money, too much arrogance, and none of the values he'd raised her and Gary to hold on to.

Jenna didn't know what it was about Blake that fascinated her so. If she did consider marrying him—

As upsetting as her discussion with her father had been, her visit to B.J.'s parents this afternoon hadn't gone much smoother. They were in shock, trying to absorb the fact she wasn't having B.J.'s baby. B.J.'s mom had cried because this child would have been an enduring link to her son. As she tried to console Charlene, Jenna's own heart had felt torn apart.

Suddenly, loud banging started in the hall outside Jenna's apartment, and at first she couldn't figure out exactly where it was coming from. Then she realized someone was pounding on Ramona's door.

The pounding turned into shouts. "Ramona, let me in. You can't keep me locked out forever."

The voice was slurred and Jenna realized it was Joe's. He'd obviously been drinking. Again there was pounding and more shouting and then the sound of something hard bashing Ramona's door, wood on wood.

Jenna jumped out of bed and flew into her bathroom. She and Ramona had conversed through the thin walls before when she'd been sick and Ramona wondered if she needed help. As she went to the wall between her apartment and Ramona's, she could hear Trina crying.

"Ramona," she called frantically. "Are you all right?"

"I'm okay" came the reply. "I called 911, but there's an accident on the highway and all the service cars are at the scene. They're going to try to get someone out here as soon as they can, but—"

There was more banging and then the sound of wood splintering.

"Hold on," Jenna said, "I'll call someone else."

Running into her bedroom, she snatched the cordless phone from the bedside stand. She could call Rafe but it would take him fifteen minutes to get here from the Rocky R. She could call her father…

Almost without conscious thought she dialed Blake's number. She'd memorized it.

He answered on the second ring. "Winston."

He sounded preoccupied and she wondered if she'd

interrupted a romantic interlude. She couldn't think about that now. "Blake, it's Jenna."

"What's wrong?" he asked tersely, knowing she wouldn't be calling at this hour unless something was.

"Joe Scarpato, Ramona's boyfriend, is outside her door pounding and shouting. He's hitting the door with something. I don't know what—a baseball bat, maybe. She called 911, but they're out on an accident call—"

"Stay in your bedroom with the door locked. Don't come out. Got it?"

If it weren't for the baby, she might have tried to talk with Joe and reason with him. But since she'd become pregnant, she looked at the world and danger differently. "I'll be in the bathroom. I can talk to Ramona in there."

"I'm on my way," he said.

When Jenna returned to the bathroom, she told Ramona she'd called Blake. Trina was still crying, as scared as her mother, and Jenna wished she could really do something for them.

The sound of wood splintering on wood reverberated again. The minutes ticked by so slowly she felt morning might come before Blake got there. Although it seemed like eons, she was sure only five to ten minutes had passed before she heard Joe shout at someone. Then there was a thump and all was quiet.

What had happened? Had Joe hit Blake over the head with a baseball bat?

The sound of a siren broke the night's stillness outside. Although she'd known what Blake had told her to do was the best idea, she said to Ramona, "I'm going to check the hall."

"No, Jenna!" Ramona shouted through the wall.

"It's quiet. I have to see what happened...if Blake's okay. The police are coming."

Hurrying to her door, Jenna could see nothing through the peephole. Lifting the chain lock, she opened the door a crack. Blake had Joe pinned in some kind of hold—his forearm was across Joe's chest and he had the man's other arm twisted behind his back. A baseball bat lay on the floor.

Two policemen rushed from the stairs into the hall. Blake said, "Everything's fine now, officers."

Seeing Jenna, Blake frowned and nodded for her to go back inside her apartment. But she came out into the hall instead, went to Ramona's battered door and called her name.

An hour later, one officer had read Joe his rights, handcuffed him and taken him to the cruiser. The other officer took Ramona's, Blake's and Jenna's statements. He was all-business and stern, questioning Jenna as much as Ramona. Blake hovered nearby, standing over Jenna, and she was glad he was there.

Ramona had gone to get Trina a glass of juice and had come back into Jenna's apartment as the officer closed his notebook. A few minutes later he was gone and Ramona was thanking Blake for his help.

"You shouldn't stay here," he told her seriously. "He'll probably be out tomorrow."

"Joe's not like that when he doesn't drink. I would never have dated him if he was. But I know I can't take any chances. I called a friend in Oregon. Joe doesn't know her. She told me before she could get me a job in the secretarial pool in her company. I'm going to pack, get a few hours' sleep, then drive Trina up there at daybreak. I have no family here, nothing to keep me.'' She looked at Jenna. ''I'll miss *you*, though.''

The two women hugged, knowing they might not see each other ever again. ''You take care of yourself,'' Ramona said to Jenna, her eyes moist.

''I will. Write to me, okay? Let me know how you're doing.''

Ramona took a slip of paper out of her pocket where she'd jotted her friend's name, address and phone number. ''Here's where I'll be staying for a while until I get a new apartment.''

The two women hugged again and then Ramona gathered up Trina and her glass of juice from the sofa and carried the little girl out into the hall. At Jenna's door, they both waved and tears came to Jenna's eyes. She was going to miss them. They'd become good friends.

Turning to face Blake, she swiped a tear away. ''I'm sorry I got you involved in this. We should have just waited for the police. You could have gotten hurt.'' Everything had happened so fast, but as she thought about it now, her hands began to tremble.

''I had twenty pounds and four inches on him. Besides that, I know how to disarm and diffuse.''

''Still...'' She put her hand to her brow, feeling a little dizzy.

''Jenna?'' Blake asked.

She waved his concern away. ''I'm fine.'' She took hold of the back of the chair. ''I just need to sit down for a few minutes.''

In an instant Blake was by her side. He swore, then mumbled, ''Too much commotion. Maybe I should call your doctor.''

''I have an appointment on Tuesday. It's just late and I was scared.'' She shivered and knew it was simply reaction to everything that had happened.

Blake saw it and crouched down before her, taking her hands in his. ''Jenna, I want you to come home with me.''

She shook her head. ''I can't.''

''Because of your father? For goodness' sake, Jenna, you have to do what's best for you and the baby. It's not safe here.''

''They took Joe to jail.''

''Just for tonight. He'll be out and looking for Ramona.''

''Not when he's sober.''

''And who knows how long he'll be sober? When he can't find Ramona, he'll come looking for you. He knows you're friends. He knows *you'll* know where she is.''

Jenna hadn't thought about that—there had been so many things to think about.

Pressing his point home, he insisted, ''You'll be cool and comfortable in my guest bedroom. You won't have to worry about preparing meals, and you can rest whenever you need to.''

After thinking about everything that had happened over the past few days—how Blake had treated her with tenderness and gentleness, how he wanted to be a full-time father, how he was determined to be involved in every minute of his baby's life, how she felt so alone here and afraid that Joe Scarpato would return—Blake's plan for her sounded heavenly. If nothing else, she needed a few days free from stress to get to know Blake better, to pull herself together and make the right decisions.

"I'll come home with you," she finally conceded. At her words, she saw the elation in Blake's eyes, the satisfaction, and also the relief.

He leaned forward then and kissed her forehead. It should have been fleeting and chaste and not mattered at all, but she could feel the touch of his lips all the way to her toes.

As he leaned back, he murmured, "That's my girl."

When she gazed into his eyes, her breath caught. Was she becoming Blake's girl?

Chapter Seven

Jenna parked her car along the circular drive, went up the stairs and opened the heavy door to Blake's house. It still felt odd coming in like this as if she belonged here. Blake had done everything he could to make her as comfortable as possible. She hadn't seen him that much, though. They'd taken some meals together, and whenever they did, she could see that one question in his eyes.

Are you going to accept my proposal?

She didn't know what she was going to do yet.

Yesterday she'd gone to church and had dinner with her father and Gary. It was no secret that her father was unhappy with the idea that she was staying at Blake's and didn't hesitate to tell her so. This afternoon after she'd finished work in his office, he'd tried to convince her again to move into the parsonage if she didn't feel safe at her apartment. But she knew that was the wrong decision to make for herself and the baby.

Passing the kitchen, she waved to Marilyn, then headed for the porch that had become her refuge along with her room. She felt very comfortable in both places. Her knitting bag sat on the table next to one of the chairs, the magazines Blake had bought concerning parenting were scattered across the low coffee table. She'd looked through them this morning before she'd left.

After she sank onto the cushioned wicker rocker, she rested her head against the high back and thought about how pleasant it would be to rock a baby out here. This would make a wonderful playroom if Blake took some of the furniture away.

When she closed her eyes, she told herself it would only be for a moment. Then she'd go freshen up before dinner.

It seemed no time passed at all until she heard Blake's voice ask, "Jenna? Do you want to take a nap in your room?"

Opening her eyes, she glanced at her watch and realized she'd fallen asleep for half an hour. That happened often when she didn't rest in the afternoon. Sitting up straight, she took a deep breath and inhaled a trace scent of Blake's cologne. He was still wearing a dress shirt and trousers, and she guessed he hadn't been home long.

"No, I don't need a nap," she said with a smile, inordinately glad to see him. "If I sleep now, I won't sleep tonight. I was just dozing for a little while."

He'd tugged off his tie and opened the top three buttons of his shirt collar. He looked virile and sexy, and she felt her body hum from his near proximity.

"I brought you something." His smile was boyish. She caught his excitement. "What?"

Producing a quart container of ice cream, he turned it so she could see the flavor—her favorite, peanut butter fudge ripple.

"How did you know?" she asked, astonished.

"I asked Gary."

"When did you talk to Gary?"

"A little while ago."

"You called him to find out what ice cream I like?"

"I called him to ask him what kind of special treats you liked. This was on the list, along with strawberry cheesecake."

Delight and warmth filled her because Blake had gone to all that trouble.

"I got something else this afternoon, too," Blake continued with the same enthusiasm. "Don't move and I'll bring it in."

Curious now, she stood and was crossing the room to the door when Blake came in carrying a four-foot-high fuzzy white teddy bear.

More than delight made her throat tighten. Looking up at him, she knew her smile couldn't begin to convey what she felt. "Oh, Blake. It's adorable."

"Do you want to keep it in your room?" he asked. "Until there's a nursery to put it in."

There were two ways she could plan for this baby. She could plan alone, find an apartment, know she'd only see her child half the time...or she could plan for this child with Blake, knowing she'd have full custody along with him. If she married Blake, she wouldn't have the kind of marriage she'd had with B.J. Just being in the same room with Blake Winston shook her up. One look from those intense gray eyes could speed up her pulse and make her heart pound. She already knew he'd want his own way on many issues, but she also believed he'd listen. Besides all that, she could concentrate on paying off her debts, not worry about next month's rent, or their child's college education.

"I made a decision about your proposal," she said suddenly.

Blake went perfectly still, then set the teddy bear on a wicker chair. When he faced her, his mouth was a tight line. The nerve worked in his jaw, and she could see her answer was all-important to him. That made her even more sure she was doing the right thing.

"First, though, I have to ask you... Are you sure this is what you want? I won't take marriage lightly, Blake. Those vows mean something to me. In a way, I still feel married to B.J. and you're going to have to be patient with me. Can you be patient?"

"If marrying you means having access to my child whenever I want it, I can be patient. For a while. I expect to have a real marriage, Jenna."

To *her* a real marriage meant sharing everything from breakfast to her partner's most innermost thoughts, but she knew Blake meant something very different.

As he slid both of his hands under her hair and gently stroked her neck, he made himself abundantly clear. "I won't be a monk, and I don't intend to be unfaithful. I think we already have chemistry. It's just a matter of whether you'll give into it or not." Proving that to her, he tilted her lips up to his.

She thought about resisting...she *really* did—because she knew he was going to do this to prove a point. But there was something raw in his eyes, something primal, and it touched a match to something primal in her.

Yet whatever the hunger inside of Blake, he obviously controlled it. Instead of taking her lips, he kissed her cheek. Tremors of desire rippled through her then as his lips followed a path under her ear and down her neck.

"Blake," she moaned weakly.

"This is what chemistry's all about, Jenna…letting it burn, going deeper into it." Then his mouth was along her neck, at the pulse point, and she couldn't help herself from leaning back to give him greater access.

His voice was seductive as he added, "You're a beautiful woman, gentle and soft with a passion inside even you don't know about."

When he stopped speaking, his lips came down on hers. Talking, let alone thinking, was out of the question. The hot demand of Blake's tongue both shocked and fascinated her. As he took the kiss deeper and explored more thoroughly, she found herself holding on to him as if he were the only strong, safe port in her world. The kiss was a pure explosion of desire, and it seemed to last forever. All of the sensations were so thrilling and so new that they wrapped around her, sealing her to him, making her realize a marriage to him couldn't be anything *but* real.

Jenna had always thought herself a sedate lady, but now she felt wild yearnings. They scared her, yet intrigued her.

Her blouse buttoned down the front. She felt Blake shift, felt his hand on her skin, and then she realized the buttons were becoming undone. She was lost in the kiss because everything he was doing felt so wonderful.

His palm covered her breast almost reverently, then his thumb teased back and forth across her nipple. Through the fabric of her bra, the sensation was excruciatingly sensual. When he freed her breast from the cup, her breath hitched. Her breasts were larger now than they'd ever been and she'd never thought she'd be proud of that. Yet she was as Blake caressed her. She could feel every sensation deep inside of her. Never before had her body been so ready for union—

No! screamed in her head. She was still wearing B.J.'s wedding ring. She still wanted to be carrying his child, didn't she?

With a small cry, she tore away from Blake, from his mouth and from his hands. Urgently she righted her clothes. "I can't do this. Not yet."

The naked hunger in Blake's eyes made her take a step back. As if he realized he'd let her see it, he closed his eyes for a moment and took a deep breath. Then he took her by her shoulders. "Don't be afraid of it, Jenna. It's the reason I asked you to marry me."

"But the baby…"

"Yes, I want my child. With any other woman, I would have fought in the courts for it. But you're not just any woman. You'll make a wonderful mother, and as I've just shown you, I think we'll be good together."

Blake hadn't mentioned love or feelings or sharing. His criteria for a good marriage *was* much different from hers. But without marriage, he definitely had the upper hand—he had the money and the influence and the power. She held no illusions about that. And she wasn't willing to risk losing her child on the whim of a judge.

"Blake, I can't give myself to you until I feel—"

"Don't wrap yourself up in romantic illusions. Didn't you *feel* when I kissed you?"

She certainly had. "I don't mean that kind of feeling."

"That kind of feeling is something we can build on."

"Have you built on it before?" she asked bluntly.

"I haven't wanted to. And the truth is—" He stopped.

"And the truth is?" she repeated, wanting him to go on.

"Never mind. It doesn't matter. What matters is that we want this partnership and we want this marriage. It will be best for you, me and the baby. Isn't that what you decided?"

What had just happened shocked her. She'd never felt wanton before, never abandoned herself to passion. Her head and her values had always stood guard over her heart. Yet if she married Blake, everything they did in their marriage bed would be appropriate.

"I have decided to marry you because I want my child to have two parents who are in his life twenty-four hours a day, seven days a week. I am agreeing to marry you because I can't afford to go to court, and I will *not* lose this baby. I'm marrying you because I think we have a lot to teach each other. But I can't just jump in with both feet. I'm not that type of person. That's why I asked if you can be patient."

"What do you think you can teach me, Jenna?" He seemed to find the concept intriguing.

"I'm hoping I can teach you to trust me. I'm hoping I can teach you about sharing who you are."

He shook his head. "If sharing means you expect me to turn myself inside out to you, you can forget that one. I don't give anyone that kind of power. I did that with a woman a long time ago, and I learned a lesson from it. So…as far as the teaching goes, you might have to just forget about that and settle for teaching our child.''

His words made her sad, but whether he knew it or not, he was already sharing little bits of himself now and then, and she hoped that would continue. That hope was what led her to say yes to his proposal. She wasn't going to argue with him about this. That wouldn't get her anywhere. ''We'll *both* teach our child.''

Studying her carefully now, he decided, ''I think we should get married as soon as possible. Do you want your father to marry us?''

''I don't think he would. He doesn't approve of anything about us being together. He gave me a lecture today on how inappropriate it was for me to be staying with you, how the town was going to talk about it.''

''That's an even better reason to get married quickly. How would you like to drive up to Reno. Ever been there?''

''Not since I was a teenager.''

''All right. I'll make reservations. Did you say you have a doctor's appointment tomorrow?''

''Yes, in the morning,'' she replied, her head spinning with the speed of what she'd set in motion.

''What if I take you and then we'll get married?''

''Oh, but I wanted to get a dress or something….''

''After your appointment I'll drive you wherever you want to go and we'll leave from there.''

She'd seen a creamy lace dress in a maternity shop in Sacramento that she knew would be perfect.

''All right,'' she said slowly. She'd made her decision and now she'd go forward with it and everything it would mean to her life...and her child's. Yet as reality sank in, she realized she'd never thought she'd be getting married again.

"What's wrong?" Blake asked as he studied her.

She shook her head as tears came to her eyes.

Unbelievably, he seemed to understand. "We're doing the right thing. You'll see."

She hoped she was doing the right thing. But she wouldn't know if it was or not until she was in the middle of it. All of her life she'd taken the safe, cautious route and now she was veering off that course. Yet her instincts told her this was the best decision to make. If her instincts were wrong...she'd deal with the consequences.

When Blake told Jenna to choose a wedding chapel as they drove into Reno, she finally saw one that looked less commercial than the others. It was called the Blue Dove, and at least it had a small white spire that resembled a church. Her father would disapprove heartily of this elopement, but she wanted it to be a fait accompli before she told him. He'd have to recognize a marriage by a justice of the peace even in Nevada.

The honeymoon suite in the finest hotel in Reno was sumptuous in its blue velvet and cream satin appointments. She'd never stayed in such luxury. But as she dressed for her wedding in the luxurious bathroom with the Roman tub, she knew she and Blake wouldn't be enjoying the luxury as they should. There was a tension between them today. He'd been as friendly and polite as always, but she felt the restraint in his manner, the guardedness in his tone. Neither of them knew what to really expect from this marriage, and whether Blake would admit it or not, she suspected he was in turmoil about it, too.

He glanced over at her often on their way to the courthouse where they obtained the marriage license. He'd played music on the CD player on their drive to Reno, and they hadn't had to make conversation. Now, however, the silence in the car underlined the serious- ness of what they were about to do.

Fortunately the line at the courthouse wasn't long and they were on their way to the Blue Dove a half hour later. After Blake slipped the car into a slot at the chapel's parking lot, he said, "I have to get something from the trunk."

Without waiting for him, she stepped out of the car into the sunlight.

When Blake joined her, he presented her with a nosegay of pink roses. "I thought you might like to carry this." His voice was gruff.

"Oh, Blake! How thoughtful of you. Thank you." As she bent her head and smelled the roses, she swal- lowed hard. The petals were cool. He must have kept the bouquet in a cooler in the trunk. Blake Winston was such a mixture of gentleness and guardedness.

"You look beautiful," he murmured.

The folds of ivory lace gracefully draped over her tummy and fell to her calves. "Thank you," she said again, feeling inordinately shy. When she looked up into his eyes, she remembered everything that had hap- pened yesterday, how she'd felt in his arms. But she couldn't let herself enjoy any of it...because of her father...her memories of B.J....

I'm doing this for the baby, she reminded herself once again.

"Is something wrong?" he asked.

She shook her head. "Just jittery, I guess." Trying to keep her voice light, she added, "I don't get married every day."

Holding the bouquet of flowers in her right hand, she clutched her small purse with her left. Her gaze fell to her plain gold wedding band, the wedding band B.J. had put on her finger.

"I bought rings while you were shopping for your dress."

So she wouldn't feel rushed, Blake had dropped her off at the maternity shop and told her to call his cell phone. She had done that, thinking he had errands of his own to run. She hadn't even considered the fact he might be buying flowers and wedding rings.

After carefully placing her bouquet on the hood of the car, she slipped off her gold band. With Blake watching, she opened her purse and slipped the band into the small zippered section inside.

Blake's eyes were an indecipherable dark gray as he took a blue velvet box out of his sports coat pocket and opened it. Both bands were set with a row of diamonds.

She looked up at him with surprise. "They're very beautiful and...elaborate."

"I thought you might like something more unusual than a plain band."

"They're...they're lovely, Blake." Her voice was shaky, and she knew he could hear that because his lips tightened. "I guess I'm just used to the...basics," she added, picking up her bouquet again. She wanted to appreciate the wedding bands, yet felt the loss of the one B.J. had placed on her finger.

"I hope it fits," he muttered. "But it will do the

trick for today. We can always get it sized. Are you ready to go in?''

His tone was brisk now and she was afraid she'd offended him. But she didn't know what to do about that. Everything felt so awkward today. It had to get better.

Yet nothing got better. In fact, everything got a lot worse.

When they stepped inside the chapel, Jenna realized it wasn't any different from the ones with the placards out front. In the lobby, there was a case of rings for couples who bought them at the last minute, bouquets of artificial flowers, CDs to use for the ceremony, and even plastic-encased descriptions of package ceremony A, B or C.

As they stood studying them, Blake asked, ''Which one do you want?''

The least expensive package was a five-minute ceremony. The most expensive package included music and a white aisle runner. ''It doesn't matter,'' she said softly, remembering her father's church where she'd married B.J., the scent of fresh flowers, her friends and family all around her.

After a cautious glance at her, Blake pointed to package C. ''We'll take this one. It seems to have every-thing.''

Everything except the true love, deep commitment and soul-searing promises that had been essential elements of her first wedding day, she thought.

As Blake lay in the dark on the honeymoon suite's fold-out sofa, he knew he'd handled everything wrong. He didn't know what he could have done differently, but obviously Jenna was upset, and he felt raw. He supposed this wedding today wasn't much different than his would have been nineteen years ago if he and Danielle had managed to elope. Except then it would have been exciting, a lark, a beginning. Preston Howard had squelched their future when he'd had Blake pulled in for kidnapping. Howard had had contacts in the police department and the charge had been meant to scare Blake away from Danielle for good. Although Danielle's father later had the arrest warrant dropped, Blake hadn't even thought of going near a wedding chapel since then.

After he plumped his pillow for the third time, he wished he could read Jenna's mind. She'd been so quiet after the wedding. Although she'd tried to make conversation throughout dinner, he could see it was an effort. Marrying him had been more difficult for her than she'd imagined, he guessed. He remembered the emotion in her eyes when she'd removed her plain gold wedding band.

A thought suddenly struck him as he thought of the old adage that history repeated itself. Jenna's father didn't approve of him, either. Batting two for two.

Trying to relax every muscle in his body took concentration, especially when Jenna was less than thirty feet away in a white cotton nightgown. He'd gone for a walk so she could comfortably get herself ready for bed. Yet when he'd returned, he'd seen the fabric against her creamy skin and noticed the little pink roses across the bodice as she'd read in bed. At least that's what she'd pretended to do. He hadn't seen her turn one page.

Now he heard her stirring and he realized she couldn't sleep, either. A few moments later, he heard her sheet rustle, then she found her robe and crossed to the balcony door. Opening it quietly, she stepped outside.

With a groan of frustration and exasperation, he sat up, then followed Jenna to the balcony. When he joined her, she was standing at the white railing, looking down over the pool.

"Jenna?" he asked cautiously.

Turning, she faced him. "I couldn't sleep."

Her hair soft and falling around her face, she looked like an angel standing there in white. Desire kick-started and he reminded himself he was only out here to find out what she was thinking. "What's wrong? You're obviously upset."

She looked surprised, as if she thought she'd been doing an excellent job of hiding it. "I'm sorry."

"There's nothing to be sorry about. This is awkward for both of us." He'd never really cared what anybody else thought before, but now he wanted to know what was on Jenna's mind.

"Yes, it is," she admitted. "I'm not used to wearing a nightgown in front of a practical stranger." She fingered her wedding band. "And the wedding today…"

"What about the wedding?" he asked gruffly.

"I guess it's just the temporary feel of everything here—choosing a chapel as if it's a restaurant, buying a packaged wedding, having an absolute stranger for a witness. The justice of the peace's wife was nice, but…"

"You didn't want your father to marry you," he said evenly.

"No, I didn't. But maybe I should have brought Gary along. I don't know. It was just so different from when B.J. and I—" She stopped abruptly.

So this was the crux of it. She was making comparisons. How often did she compare him to B.J.? How often did she think about the life she'd had in preference to the one she might have? And if they ever *did* sleep together, would she be comparing performances, too?

"You knew this would be different, Jenna. You knew we were getting married because of the baby." His voice came out sterner than he'd intended.

When she looked up at him, her eyes were moist. "I know." Her gaze fell to his bare chest, and he thought he saw her cheeks flush in the hotel's back lighting. "That doesn't make it any easier," she added. "We're going to have to grow into this, Blake. But I think it's going to take more time than either of us thought."

What she was saying was clear. She wasn't ready for an intimate relationship between them and might never be. "You're just upset tonight. Maybe in the morning—"

She shook her head. "It will all still be there. I'm not saying I regret marrying you, but I'm going to need time to absorb it all."

He was angry and frustrated without knowing all the reasons why. "What you're saying is, when we get back, you want a separate bedroom. You don't want me making advances. You don't want to be a real wife."

"It's not that black and white, Blake. I don't know how I'm going to feel in a few weeks...or when the baby's born...or after that."

"Fine. Don't worry about it, Jenna. If you can't be a wife, at least I'll have a nanny for the baby."

Her eyes widened and she looked wounded. He wanted so badly to take her into his arms and simply hold her, but he didn't think she was ready for even that.

"I'm going to turn in," he said tersely. "We'll leave after breakfast in the morning. I have work to do when we get back."

And before he touched her, before he made one of those advances she was fearing, he went back inside the honeymoon suite, wondering if any other married couple who had stayed here had ever had less of a honeymoon.

Chapter Eight

As water from the tiered fountain cascaded over rocks the following afternoon, Jenna wandered the gardens behind Blake's house, stopping to smell a beautiful red rose. She wondered how her life had gotten so confused. One day she and B.J. were perfectly happy, just waiting for their future to unfold the way they wanted it. The next, he'd been diagnosed with cancer and the roller coaster ride had begun. She'd had no choice but to move to an apartment because she couldn't keep up with the bills.

Continuing on the crushed marble path, she knew her decision to have B.J.'s baby might have been an unusual one. Still, it had felt so right. She'd known her father would come around as soon as he saw his grandchild.

And now...

The wrought-iron bench under a live oak beckoned

to her. She sat on it, twisting Blake's ring on her finger. When he'd come out to the balcony last night, she'd had the irrational urge to dive into his arms, to let him take her to bed and make her his. Yet she'd known him so short a time, and memories of B.J. were still so much a part of her. She felt guilty because her feelings for Blake were growing stronger each day. Somehow that felt like a betrayal of B.J.'s love. She also felt guilty because she'd never experienced with B.J. the commanding sexual pull she experienced toward Blake. It had been the guilt that had made her back away from Blake last night, had urged her to put distance between them until she got it all sorted out. How could she be Blake's wife when she still felt married to B.J.? When she'd tried to express that to Blake…it had become muddled and he'd felt as if she were reneging on their bargain. Was she?

After they'd returned from Reno yesterday, Blake had gone to Sacramento and she hadn't seen him for the rest of the day. She hadn't seen him this morning, either. He'd been up and gone before she'd had breakfast.

This morning had been almost as difficult as last night. After she'd fortified herself with toast and a glass of milk, she'd driven to the parsonage and told her father she'd married Blake. He'd been stunned and asked her if she'd lost her mind. She'd left before he finished his dire predictions of how unhappy she would be. She didn't see how she could be any more unhappy with Blake than she would be giving up even partial custody of her child.

Somehow they would work out the terms of their marriage.

The growl of an engine alerted Jenna. That was

Blake's car. She heard a second car, too, and decided to go in to investigate. When she stepped inside the kitchen, she found Blake taking two tumblers from the cupboard.

"Hi," she said carefully, not knowing exactly what to say next.

He put one glass under the ice maker in the refrigerator door. "Do you know where Marilyn is?"

"She told me she was running errands this afternoon. Why?"

"Al Bailey and I are having a meeting in my study. We didn't have lunch yet, and I was hoping she could throw something together."

"I can do that," Jenna offered quickly.

There were a few beats of heavy silence before Blake picked up a second glass to fill with ice. "You don't have to. I'll send out."

Unable to bear the tension between them, she caught his arm. "I'm serious. I'll find something to make. From what I've seen so far, Marilyn keeps the refrigerator well stocked. I'd like to. I mean..." She didn't know exactly how to put this tactfully. "I *am* your wife."

The noise of ice falling into a tumbler punctuated her words. After he set both glasses on the counter, he said, "Maybe you should give me a list of the duties that encompasses."

His tone and reference to their disastrous wedding night made her angry, and the tension inside her burst free. "I've known you for *ten* days. *Ten* days! We married so neither of us would have to be apart from this child. So don't act like a bridegroom who's been engaged for a year and expected to score on his wedding night."

Blake's eyebrows shot up at that, and she realized she'd possibly shocked him. Well, she was going to be shocking a lot of people if her life kept taking the turns it had taken lately.

"You know how to throw a good left hook and land it where it matters." He didn't look happy about it, but she had the feeling he respected her for standing up to him.

As he leaned against the counter, he seemed to relax a bit. "I'm not kidding about that list, Jenna. We both need an idea of where we stand and what kind of boundaries we're setting, or we'll be crossing horns all the time."

She could see he was serious. "Why don't we start out with the easy things? There's no reason why I can't fix something for lunch and bring it in to your office. I'm comfortable in the kitchen, and I love to cook."

"Are you suggesting we make this list as we go?" His tone was wry as he considered it.

"I guess I am."

Eyeing her cautiously, he asked, "Can you add hostessing to your list? I've invited two associates and their wives for an evening on the *Suncatcher*. I'll have everything catered, but I'd like you to act as hostess. We could spend the night on the boat if you'd like."

"My condition wouldn't be…awkward?"

He crossed his arms in what she realized was a defensive gesture. "Your condition is a matter of record and when we have a baby, everybody's going to know about it. The arrival of my firstborn won't be awkward for me. Will it be awkward for you?"

"As long as we don't tell everybody about how this all came about, it should be fine," she replied.

Uncrossing his arms, he approached her and stopped

about a foot away. "I promise, Jenna, I won't tell anyone about the mix-up at the clinic unless you agree to it."

"You don't have any close friends you want to tell?"

"I don't have close friends."

"Aren't you lonely?" The question popped out before she could catch it. She couldn't imagine life without her friends.

"I'm too busy to be lonely. If I wanted to work twenty-four hours a day, there would be enough to do. I know it's not the same thing, but I'm as serious about what I do as you are about teaching. Matter of fact, I'd better get to it. I'll take the lemonade in with me. If you could fix sandwiches or something, that would be great." He was looking at her as if he wanted to say more. He was looking at her as if he was trying to figure out where they were going to go from here. Then he turned away and opened the refrigerator to find the pitcher of lemonade.

Fifteen minutes later, Jenna carried two plates to Blake's office. She'd found a turkey breast Marilyn had baked along with potato salad. She'd made thick sandwiches with turkey and cheese and mustard, added the salad and a few baby carrots on the side.

Blake's office door was open. As she came upon it, she heard, "We have to take this threat seriously. I know Evanston thinks there's no substance to it. That's why he doesn't want the authorities brought in. But we have to act as if there *is* substance to it. We can't take any chances—his life and our reputation are on the line."

Fear stabbed Jenna as she heard the word *threat.* Is that why security would be tighter than usual at Evanston's fund-raiser? She'd heard that lots of politicians, as well as celebrities, received threats that had no actual basis. But somehow this sounded more serious and she wondered if Blake would be in harm's way. Then she dismissed the thoughts. He was the head of security running the operation and would be in the background.

So Blake would know she was outside the door, she clinked the two plates together, then stepped inside.

Blake stood when she came in, took one plate from her and said, "Al's can go on the desk. Al, this is my wife, Jenna. Jenna, Al Bailey, my right-hand man."

Al Bailey had bright red hair and very green eyes. He had the appearance of a bodybuilder, looked to be near forty and was almost as tall as Blake.

"It's nice to meet you," she said with a quick smile. "I hope this is okay for lunch."

Quickly examining the sandwich, he grinned. "Turkey and mustard—my favorite. I hear congratulations are in order. You and Blake are newlyweds."

His gaze went to her tummy and she felt herself blush. She could see now that she and Blake would have two choices with strangers. They could either tell them the truth or they would think she'd conceived this baby out of wedlock and married late in the game.

"Yes, we are," she answered lightly. "But now I'm going to leave my husband to his work."

Blake came around the desk and motioned outside the door. Once there, he asked, "Do you have plans for this afternoon?"

"I'm going to call Shannon and see if she's free. I want to tell her about our marriage."

"Your lawyer's going to hit the roof."

"Not any harder than Dad did."

Blake's brow furrowed. "You told him?"

"This morning. I didn't think you'd want another scene like the last one."

"I would have gone with you, Jenna. You didn't have to do it alone."

"I thought it was better if I went alone. Gary seemed happy, though."

Examining her carefully, Blake asked, "Did your dad disown you?"

"No, but he still might…if I give it time." She gave Blake a smile. "I have to keep a sense of humor about this. I can't cry any more than I already have. Maybe it's a good thing this happened so Dad realizes I have my own life and he can't dictate it."

Blake seemed to digest that. "There's one other thing I wanted to tell you. By the end of the week, you'll have credit cards in your name. If you want to buy anything for the baby or anything else for that matter, feel free. I imagine you'll need something for the party on the boat."

"I can't let you buy me—"

When he slid his hand under her hair quickly, she hadn't even suspected he was going to do it. His gray eyes were serious. "This one's on *my* list, Jenna. You're my wife. I plan to take care of you. You'll need something with a little sparkle for the boat. Buy whatever you like. Don't worry about how much it costs. The same for the baby. Are we clear on that?"

His hand on her neck was almost a caress. The deep tugging she always felt toward him was in full force now and she had to catch her breath. She knew she had to give in to some aspects of this marriage or it would never work. Taking care of her appeared to be important to Blake, and letting him buy her an outfit to hostess a party, letting him buy things for the baby, was reasonable.

"I didn't know women wore glittery dresses on boats," she managed to say, all too distracted by the warmth of his hand on her skin.

He smiled. "These two women do. I'll take you into Sacramento if you'd rather shop there."

"I can drive," she assured him. "I bet Shannon would love to help me pick something out."

"In other words, you'd rather not have me along." His lips twitched, and she knew he wasn't taking offense.

"Sometimes you make me nervous," she confessed.

He lowered his hand to his side. "We'll have to work on that. I'd rather you felt something other than nervous."

On that note, he disappeared into his office and closed the door.

She felt a lot more than nervous when she was around Blake. But she wasn't ready to tell him that…yet.

In the galley of the *Suncatcher* after Blake's guests left Saturday night, Jenna stored the leftovers in the refrigerator, glad for something to do. Suddenly tonight, on a small scale, she'd realized what her position as Mrs. Blake Winston actually entailed and she didn't know if she was prepared for it. Just because she wore the right clothes didn't make her one of *them*. The men had stood at the helm with Blake as he piloted the boat down the river past Courtland, while Jenna conversed with the women…or tried to. On the return trip, Jenna had mostly listened.

Suddenly Blake came down the stairs and entered

the galley, so tall and handsome in his black dinner jacket and tie. His gaze fell over her emerald-green tunic top and slacks Shannon had helped her select. It was silk and seemed to shimmer under any light. Blake's colleagues' wives had worn beaded dresses, but Jenna hadn't felt out of place because of the outfit she'd chosen. She felt out of place because she didn't know anything about Blake's world.

"You didn't have a good time tonight, did you?" he asked her now.

Everything between her and Blake had gotten more intense since they'd married. All he had to do was look at her, and she could see the desire in his eyes. All he had to do was touch her, and she trembled. Tonight he'd slipped his arm around her waist a couple of times in front of his guests, leaned close and murmured in her ear. Because they were supposed to be newlyweds?

"It wasn't supposed to show," she replied softly.

"I don't think anyone noticed but me. I can tell when your smile is forced. You forced it a lot tonight. Didn't you like Mona and Debra?"

"They're lovely women."

"But?" he probed.

The galley was way too small with Blake in it. "I have nothing in common with them. They organize charity functions, plan theater presentations, serve on the boards of foundations. That's not the kind of life I live."

"It can be. You're my wife now."

It sounded like a proclamation. "I might be your wife, but I'm who I've always been. I'm not going to change just because I married you. I still want to teach."

Blake unfastened his tie, then loosened his shirt collar. "You don't seem to understand what being my wife means. You won't have to work. I'm taking over your financial responsibilities."

"I can't let you do that," she protested.

As he took a step closer, he seemed to tower over her. "Is your independence more important than peace of mind?"

She had no peace of mind when he was this close. "I don't know," she murmured. "I *do* know I can't turn all the responsibilities of my life over to you. Even if I don't *have* to work, I'm a teacher, Blake."

"You'll be teaching our son or daughter."

This man could be so frustratingly reasonable, but she had logic of her own on her side. "*You're* not going to quit your job and stop working because *you're* having a baby."

"Jenna…"

"Don't tell me it's not a valid argument."

"It's not. My work will keep both of us comfortable. Your job barely pays the bills. That's the reality of it."

Her pulse raced, and she knew she had to take a stand on this. "No. The reality is you're trying to control my life and I don't like it."

The sound of a boat horn broke the tense silence.

Blake asked, "What are you really upset about?"

"I'm *not* upset." As her voice rose, she realized she'd just proved she was.

"I think I know what it is," he continued. "The Cantrells and the Boswicks thought you and I were having an affair, and this baby and our wedding is a natural result of that."

Was she upset about that? She'd been a virgin when she'd married B.J. That's the way she'd been raised. The idea that somebody thought she was sleeping with

Blake Winston and almost having a child out of wedlock didn't sit well with her. "I know you didn't want
to go into long explanations," she said, her voice calm
now. "Neither did I. But your hand-holding and the
lovey-dovey stuff for everyone's benefit—"

Suddenly Blake was so close she could feel his body
heat. "I wasn't pretending tonight. I enjoy touching
you. This little party just gave me an excuse to do it
more often." His low voice excited her and made her
insides quiver.

"You promised not to pressure me," she managed
to say.

"Did I pressure you tonight in any way?"

Trying to step away from him, she felt her back
against the counter. "You're pressuring me now. When
you're so close, I...forget how we got into all of this."

A self-satisfied male smile played on his lips. He
didn't touch her, but he didn't have to when he seemed
to surround her with his male scent, his confident virility. "Forgetting it might be best for both of us."

Slowly she shook her head and her gaze pleaded
with him to understand. Yet she could see he didn't
and maybe never would.

With a resigned expression, he rubbed his hand
up and down the back of his neck. "It's late—almost
2:00 a.m. Are you sure you'll be okay on the boat
tonight?"

When he'd told her about this party, he'd said they
could sleep on the boat. It had seemed like an adventure—an adventure she might not have for a very long
time if she didn't take advantage of it. Once the baby
was born, her time would be consumed by their child.
Now the intimacy of the boat seemed a little too
intense, but she knew Blake was tired and she was,

too. There was no sense in driving back to Fawn Grove now.

"I'll be fine."

"I put your overnight bag in the main cabin. I'm going to read in the salon for a while. Call me if you need anything."

Before she could assure him again she'd be fine, he left the galley and she heard the door close on the second smaller bedroom, if the V-berth could be called that.

A short while later, Jenna realized the bed was big enough for her to be comfortable. The problem was— she wasn't comfortable with her feelings…with everything that was happening…or with her life. Each moment she spent with Blake bonded her to him more in some unseen way that she felt, yet couldn't understand. Her attraction to him had been so instantaneous, the pull toward him so inescapable.

How could that be? With B.J., they'd been friends for months before they'd even kissed. He'd put a roof on the parsonage and that's where she'd met him. They'd gone bike riding, attended builders shows together, watched old movies. The first time B.J. kissed her had been nothing like when Blake kissed her.

Jenna tried to ease herself onto her left side. The whole boat seemed to creak every time she turned over. She knew it had to be her imagination and the fact that Blake wasn't far away.

When the baby kicked, she sat up and turned on the light. "You're not going to let me go to sleep, are you?" she asked, knowing her thoughts as much as her child were keeping her awake. She'd brought along a novel that was still in her overnight bag. Maybe if she read for a while…

She'd just slid her feet over the side of the bed when there was a light rap on the door. "Jenna?"

"I'm awake," she called.

The door opened and Blake stood there in a pair of red jogging shorts. The rest of him was bare. She tried to take him all in at one time—the broad tanned shoulders, the black curls down the middle of his chest, his navel with another whorl of black hair...

"I thought I heard you talking. I didn't know if you might need something."

She smiled and stroked her tummy. "I was talking to the baby. I do that a lot, especially when he or she won't let me sleep."

As he stepped into the room, Blake's gaze went to her hand, then lifted to her breasts under the thin cotton gown.

Where had she put her robe? It was on the hook on the back of the door. To retrieve it, she'd have to pass him. Better to retreat. Scurrying into the bed again, she pulled the sheet up.

"Jenna," he said with a shake of his head. Then as if he understood her modesty was something she couldn't just slough off, he asked, "What calms him down?"

"Him?" she asked with a smile.

"It seemed as good a choice as any."

"I think it's a 'him,' too," she confided. "I don't know why—just a feeling."

But then she did know why and it seemed as if Blake realized it the same time she did. B.J. was gone. It was only fitting a little boy should take his place in the world.

"Maybe I should hope it's a girl," Blake muttered.

"I don't want you regretting a little boy didn't have B.J. Winton's eyes, nose or chin."

Blake's words made her heart catch. "Oh, Blake. Have we done the right thing?"

Crossing over to her then, he sank down on the bed beside her. "It will *be* the right thing if we decide it *is* the right thing. I know you can't turn off your feelings for B.J., but maybe I can make you forget them for a little while."

She could back away as she had before. She could remind herself it was too soon. She hardly knew Blake and he'd shared so little with her. Yet in other ways, he'd shared so much.

When he leaned toward her, for the moment she forgot who she was and what she should do. Her pulse leapt as her hands went to Blake's shoulders, and she couldn't help herself from exploring the muscles there.

Groaning, he bent even closer, but instead of kissing her, he simply grazed her cheek with his lips. He did it so sensually. It was such an enticement that her fingers dug into his taut skin.

"What do you want, Jenna?" he asked.

She'd never been asked that before. "A kiss," she whispered, thinking that was all, and that would be the end of it.

"I think you want more than a kiss, but we'll start with that." His husky, deep voice rushed out in a hot breath as he lifted his legs onto her bed and lay face-to-face with her. "You always smell like flowers," he murmured as his lips moved over hers, not quite taking, not quite kissing.

She couldn't understand what he wanted as she felt his tongue on her upper lip. Trying to tell him that, she stroked his back and felt him shudder. She was surprised. He was an experienced man. Even B.J. hadn't responded to her like that. Everything about sex with him had been matter of fact...expected. With Blake—

When he licked her lower lip next, she felt a quiver deep inside, a response that was like tiny bursts of pleasure. "What are you doing?" she whispered.

He smiled against her lips. "Tasting you, enjoying you, teaching you what you should really expect from a kiss. It can go on a very long time," he explained solemnly, and leaned away.

"I thought a kiss was just a kiss."

"Not with you. Not with me. Not with us. That's what I've been trying to tell you."

Then he really *was* kissing her, and she was falling...falling into a place she'd never known...falling into a man she didn't know...falling in love. It was a wisp of a thought, and she couldn't quite catch it as Blake's tongue heated her and created an excitement she'd never known before.

While he kissed her, in creatively slow, sensual strokes, his hand caressed her breast. She was aware of his fingers unbuttoning her gown. Yet she was so lost in him and the sensual haze he was weaving around her that she was most concerned with touching him, learning more about his strength, learning more about what made him who he was.

The sheet got pushed down and away from their legs. His intertwined with hers. He seemed to be touching her everywhere, and she loved all of it. It had been so long. She'd felt so alone.

She didn't feel alone now.

Her body thrummed as her sighs and moans broke through their kisses and his caresses. His hands left her breasts to caress her thigh. She felt as if she were a new woman in his arms, a different woman from the one she'd been. He was bringing her alive in ways she'd never been alive. When his fingers touched the nest between her thighs, she gasped. But it was from pleasure, not shock. She couldn't think. She could only feel. Everything Blake was doing made her feel so much. When his fingers stroked her, she felt like a shooting star, burning out of control.

Suddenly waves of pleasure began to wash over her until he touched her even more intimately, and her world burst into the deepest blue fire of physical satisfaction. Her breath came in gasps, and her whole body quivered and trembled. The climax had been more powerful than any she had ever experienced. Opening her eyes, she looked at Blake. As her breathing slowed, she realized what had happened.

"Don't think about it," he whispered close to her temple. "Just enjoy it."

She had enjoyed it, but now—

To her surprise, Blake reached for the sheet and brought it up to cover her. Then he pushed himself upright and swung his legs over the bed. "Maybe you can get some sleep now," he said gently. "I hear sex is as good as a sleeping pill."

"But we didn't—"

"No, we didn't. I wanted you to see what it could be like for us. That was just foreplay, Jenna. Imagine the main event."

She knew her cheeks were probably redder than he'd ever seen them, and she was at a complete loss for words.

"I'll see you in the morning," he said, as casually as if they'd just had a conversation about the weather.

Before she could prop herself up against the wall to

gain her equilibrium, he'd left the cabin. Closing her eyes, she staved off regret, embarrassment and guilt to remember the way it had felt to explode in Blake's arms.

Chapter Nine

Blake's office in Sacramento used to be a haven of sorts. He'd spent most of his time there. He'd even slept many nights on the camel leather couch when he'd worked late. *Home* wasn't a word he'd thought about since he was a kid. Nevertheless, since Jenna had moved into his house, it had seemed like a home. She hadn't gone around rearranging the furniture or buying new stuff. They'd moved very little of her apartment furnishings into his house...just an old rocker she'd wanted for the baby's room. The rest had gone into storage in one of the outbuildings. Still...her mere presence in the house had changed it from a building where he stopped in once in a while, to a place he looked forward returning to.

She'd kept her distance from him for the past few days, and he realized that had been part of the risk he'd taken Saturday night on the boat. That night, he'd just had the overwhelming desire to make her look at him as a man, to make her forget B.J. Winton and the memories that seemed to grip her.

And what if she does forget B.J.? a tiny, insistent voice inside of him asked. *What then?*

That was simple. She could enjoy their marriage without guilt.

He reminded himself he'd married her because of their baby. Yet if he and Jenna truly became man and wife, he wanted her to leave her thoughts of her first husband in the past.

Blake's phone rang and he reached across his desk. His receptionist told him Danielle Howard was on line three.

Danielle. A vision of how she'd looked at eighteen flashed in his mind—how she'd looked when she'd chosen her father's allowance and a college education over him. The years had put Danielle in his past, but they couldn't let him forget for a minute that Danielle had put a comfortable future high above any feelings she had for him.

He pushed line three and said neutrally, "Blake Winston."

"Blake, it's Danielle Howard. Remember me?"

How he remembered. "Sure, Danielle. I remember."

Sighing as if she expected more than that, she gave a little laugh. "I'm back in Fawn Grove after all these years. I'm living with Dad at the moment while I'm having an apartment redecorated in Sacramento. I thought maybe we could get together some time—for old times' sake."

He could go into long explanations or he could just cut this conversation short, which is what he preferred. "I'm booked up for a while. I'm going out of town until the weekend and then I have...other commitments.''

''Are you still angry with me after all these years?'' Actually, she sounded hopeful that he might be, as if that proved she was unforgettable.

''What you did changed the course of my life,'' he said honestly.

''You mean what I *didn't* do. I didn't marry you.''

''Your decision to stay in your father's good graces pushed me to make a success of my life. So I should probably thank you for that.''

''You owe what you are today to me?'' she asked, intrigued by the thought.

''Some of it. But my leaving Fawn Grove also pushed my father into a place that led him to commit suicide.''

There was stunned silence for a few moments. ''Blake, I'm sorry. I didn't know.''

''I guess your father didn't send the local paper to your dorm.''

''No, he didn't. Blake, this isn't something we should talk about on the phone. Can we get together?''

''We don't have anything to talk about, Danielle. I hope this move back here is the right one for you. Goodbye.''

When Blake hung up the phone, he had a bitter taste in his mouth. As a teenager, he'd been so impressed with the homecoming queen that he hadn't been able to believe his luck when Danielle had shown an interest in him. She'd loved riding on the back of his bike with him, and he'd felt like the king of Fawn Grove having her there. But the night they'd tried to elope, Danielle's personality had become clear to him when she'd turned her back on him and gone home with her father. She'd always wanted what she couldn't have; she'd always wanted what made everyone stand up and take notice. She'd always wanted to please her father no matter what the cost, and he suspected that was still the case.

Jenna, on the other hand, had gone against her father's wishes and married him. But she'd had driving reasons behind that decision. She didn't want to lose any part of her life with her child, and she'd learned about the security he could offer her. He had the feeling when push came to shove, she'd do everything she could to please *her* father, too.

Abruptly, Blake realized he'd never cared whether his father approved of what he did or not. After his mom died, his father had withdrawn and ignored Blake. His drunken stupors kept him anesthetized. Blake had thought his father didn't care, that his father didn't need him. By committing suicide, his dad had shown him that he'd needed Blake more than Blake had ever known, and his son had let him down. Blake should have stayed and yanked his father back to the land of the living. He should have dragged his dad to an A.A. meeting. The guilt of not doing or being enough still crawled out of dark corners when Blake least suspected it.

His phone buzzed again. It was his secretary confirming his flight reservations to Seattle. As he took down the information, he realized he'd have to leave earlier than he'd planned. He wouldn't get home again today to see Jenna. Would she miss his presence in her life for a couple of days or would she be relieved?

He dialed his home number and Marilyn answered and took the cordless phone to Jenna. ''She's on the porch having lunch,'' Marilyn told him.

He knew it was Jenna's favorite room in the house.

"Hi, Blake," his wife answered. "Is something wrong?"

"No, nothing's wrong. One of my meetings was moved up so I have to fly out sooner than I expected. I wanted to let you know I'll be leaving in an hour."

"Oh."

Was that disappointment he heard?

"Don't you have to pack?"

"I keep extra clothes here and a travel bag. This isn't unusual. Let me give you the name of the hotel where I'll be staying." He waited while she wrote it all down.

"Are you sure Shannon doesn't mind taking over for me tonight?" He didn't like missing the parenting class.

"She doesn't mind. We'll have a girls' night out." After a short pause she asked, "Do you know when you'll be back?"

"Sometime on Saturday."

"I probably won't be here when you get home."

That gave him pause for a moment. "You have plans?"

"There's a carnival at school. I told them I'd help out."

"Help out how?"

"Don't worry. It's nothing taxing. I'm going to supervise the servers for the pot roast dinner and help make salad. That kind of thing."

"No lifting, Jenna." This worry he felt over her and their child was new to him, but he accepted it as part of being a father.

"I have friends here who will watch over me. They won't let me overdo."

Probably old friends she and B.J. had known for years. "How long will you be there?"

"Until evening. A local country band will be playing. They're one of my favorites."

He hated being out of contact with her. That was new, too. "If you have your phone with you, I'll call you when I get in."

"All right. But don't worry about me, okay? I'll be fine."

How often did she tell him that, as if it was her banner of independence. She was a strong woman, but she was pregnant now and that made a difference.

"I'll see you on Saturday," he said.

"Saturday," she repeated, and then clicked off the phone.

Jetting away had never bothered him before. That was his life, his work. He didn't like the fact that it bothered him now.

When Blake returned on Saturday, it was almost 5:00 p.m. He'd tried calling Jenna on her cell phone, but she didn't answer. It hadn't taken him long to admit he'd missed her.

He'd had women in his life over the years who'd filled a physical need. They'd slept with him and gone to the theater with him and had dinner with him at the finest restaurants. But he'd never missed any of them when he was away from them. Jenna wasn't even sharing his bed, yet her presence somehow surrounded him.

Hurrying to the kitchen, he informed Marilyn he was going to Parkview Elementary School for the carnival and she wouldn't need to prepare supper.

Her curious look made him defensive. "Jenna's there. I don't want her to overdo it."

"That one wouldn't do anything to hurt the baby."

He believed that. Nevertheless, Jenna was good-

hearted and hard-working. She might not keep her vol-
unteerism to a reasonable level.

When he arrived at the school, the parking lot was
filled with concession stands, kiddie rides and residents
of Fawn Grove milling around. When he saw the sign
advertising the pot roast dinner, he headed that way,
assuming he'd find the cafeteria and the kitchen.

The tables weren't filled yet in the large, institutional
room, and he guessed they'd just started serving. A
teenager carried a tray of platters to a table, and an
older woman with an apron tied around her waist was
pouring sodas into glasses of ice. Collages hung on
easels near the door to the kitchen, and Blake stopped
and studied them curiously.

In bright red letters, he read, Past Carnivals. There
were photographs of grinning kids, a clown, a minia-
ture ladybug ride, excited toddlers. He was about to
turn away when he caught sight of Jenna in a picture
on the bottom row. She was wearing a brightly colored
sundress that hugged her breasts and slim waist.
Around that waist was a man's arm, and Blake realized
he was seeing his first picture of B.J. Winton. Obviously from the way they were looking at each other,
their bond was strong. B.J. was wearing a red bandanna
on his bald head. Jenna's smile told Blake how much
she'd cared for her husband, how much she'd willed
him to live.

Turning away from the picture, his chest tight, he
entered the kitchen and spotted Jenna right away. She
was sitting at a table with a woman more pregnant than
she was, wrapping silverware in napkins. She was un-
aware of Blake as he came up behind her, and he could
hear the two women talking.

The blonde, who looked as if she could deliver at

any moment, said, "I'm glad you remembered the rec-
ipe for B.J.'s special sauce. The pot roast wouldn't
have been the same without it. Everybody who bought
a ticket would have complained."

Blake couldn't see Jenna's face, but he could hear
her response. "Making his sauce every year is another
way for me to keep his memory alive. I'm so afraid it
will fade and I'll forget the sound of his laughter, the
crinkle lines around his eyes, the way he danced the
two-step."

The blonde nodded. "I know exactly what you
mean. When my dad died, all I wanted to do was watch
those home movies over and over again. Somehow,
they take me back to him. Do you have movies or
videotapes?"

"Just of our wedding."

Blake's chest tightened even more when he realized
Jenna sounded sad about that. Did she wish she could
bury herself in memorabilia of B.J. Winton so she'd
never forget anything about him or their life together?
That question lanced Blake's heart like nothing had
since his father's death.

Not as engrossed in their conversation now, the
blonde caught sight of Blake. "Can I help you?" Her
gaze was assessing him in his white dress shirt, tie and
slacks. He hadn't even bothered to change.

Had Jenna told these women about their marriage?
Just how was he supposed to handle this? "I'm here
to see Jenna." He couldn't keep the edge from his tone.

At the sound of Blake's voice, Jenna turned. As she
stood, several sets of silverware dropped to the floor.
She bent to retrieve them, but Blake held her shoulder.
"I'll do it."

When he'd picked up the silverware, Jenna looked

flustered. Loosening his tie, he tugged it open and it hung under his shirt collar. "I wanted to make sure you were okay."

She looked toward the blonde. "Gladys, this is…my husband, Blake Winston. Blake, Gladys Sanders."

Gladys smiled. "It's good to meet you, Blake. Jenna told me she got married last week." In an aside, she murmured, "I think she's letting the news make the rounds slowly so people aren't shocked. I noticed her new wedding band and she told me. Congratulations."

Blake felt some of the tension ease from his shoulders. At least Jenna was telling a few people they were married.

Her face flushed, Jenna explained, "Gladys and I've kept each other from doing too much—the buddy system. I didn't realize you were going to come over here. Have you eaten anything yet?"

"No, I thought I could pick up something here."

"Pot roast or something from the concession stands?"

The pot roast with B.J. Winton's sauce didn't sound appetizing. "Do you feel like walking around the stands, or are you tied up here?"

Gladys leaned close to Jenna. "Just give me the schedule so I know who's doing what, and you take off. Realistically speaking, you shouldn't be here. You're on a honeymoon."

Jenna's cheeks reddened even more as she murmured, "I'll get the schedule."

Fifteen minutes later, Blake and Jenna were nibbling on slices of pizza as they walked around the carnival area. Blake eyed her warily. "Are you sure you're going to feel okay on that?"

She grinned like a kid. "I know it's strange, but I'm

fine with pizza. It's just spice cookies I have a problem with,'' she added.

Actually, he was grateful for those spice cookies. If she hadn't gotten sick, she might never have stayed with him the first time.

A band had been tuning up, and now the announcer came over the loudspeaker and welcomed everyone. As the rides started one by one, the band began playing a well-known country tune.

"Do you like country?" she asked.

"I've never listened to much of it. Do you want to sit on the grass? I have a blanket in the trunk of my car."

"If you promise to help me up," she said, still smiling.

"I promise," he assured her and their eyes locked as they remembered other promises. Maybe she'd missed him, too, he thought.

Breaking the moment, Blake looked away and headed for his car.

As Blake went to get the blanket, Jenna picked a spot on the grass and wondered if he'd overheard her conversation with Gladys. Although Gladys had discovered Jenna had married Blake, she tactfully hadn't pressed for details. The conversation had drifted to B.J. as it had with many of her friends. She and her husband had always invested a lot of time putting this carnival together, working the stands, volunteering in the kitchen. It was natural that people would ask her how she was doing and mention B.J.

It all seemed so complicated when it came to explanations. She hadn't told Gladys this child was Blake's. Word had gotten around that she'd decided to have B.J.'s baby. In schools especially, gossip spread like wildfire and she'd begun showing before the term was over. Kids asked questions, parents asked questions, and Jenna had told them the truth. Now she didn't know how to change everybody's perception. She certainly wasn't about to make an announcement.

As Blake returned with the blanket, she realized how glad she was to see him. But there existed an almost constant tension between them whenever they were near each other, especially after what had happened Saturday night on the boat. She'd been shocked to realize she could respond to Blake that way, so easily, without inhibitions. It had taken her the first two months of her marriage to B.J. before she could undress in front of him. With Blake, any inhibitions disintegrated whenever he touched her or kissed her. Yet she didn't feel ready to handle a real marriage to Blake. Her feelings for him were growing day by day and that unsettled her, maybe because she still didn't know where she stood with him. He wanted his child; he wanted sex. But did he want to uphold his vows with a vital commitment that would last forever?

A few minutes later as they sat on the blanket, their shoulders grazing every now and then, Jenna asked, "Was your trip successful?"

"I had a meeting with upper management in Seattle. It went okay. Sometimes I feel as if I should be three places at once."

"Can't someone else handle it?"

He gave her a wry smile. "That would require me letting go of some control. I tell myself I should. I tell myself I have good people in place. But I still try to oversee everything."

Control was important to Blake, Jenna suspected, because of his childhood when he'd had none, because of what his dad had done. She had questions about that, but the subject was so personal, she didn't feel she could bring it up without Blake opening the door.

The band was good, and in the next hour, Blake came and went with sodas and French fries. After she'd finished the last of her fries, she said, "I called Ramona last night."

"How is she?" He seemed genuinely interested.

"She and Trina are still settling in. But she has a job with a company where her friend works. They even have day care on site. She's hoping to move into an apartment of her own by the end of the summer."

"It's hard to start over," Blake said. "It's harder to change as you get older. Ramona has courage."

"We're changing our lives. Does that mean we're courageous, too?"

Gazing deeply into her eyes, he answered, "I suppose it does."

Slowly Blake leaned toward her and brushed the salt from her upper lip. She stilled at his touch, every fiber of her aware of him, aware of how he'd made her body sing. When his gray eyes darkened, she guessed he was thinking about it, too.

"Blake?" a woman's voice queried as she stepped up beside their blanket.

When Blake looked up, his whole demeanor changed. He'd rolled up his sleeves and he'd been relaxed...smiling. Now there was a tightening in his expression that Jenna didn't understand. As he stood, she felt she should, too. He held out his hand to her, and she took it as he drew her to her feet.

He didn't look happy to be making introductions. "Danielle Howard, meet my wife, Jenna Winston."

Danielle's eyes held a look of astonishment for a

moment as she looked at Jenna's tummy. Then she gave Jenna a practiced smile. "Hello."

"How did you find me?" Blake asked.

"I called your house and told your housekeeper it was urgent that I find you."

"Just why was it so urgent?"

"Dad has decided to back Nolan Constantine. He wants to have a meeting tomorrow with you and a few other people who are interested."

"You couldn't leave a message on my machine to that effect? Why are *you* asking rather than your father?"

Apparently Danielle could hold her own in any situation. Blake's questions were blunt, but she answered them easily.

"Dad thought because of our history, it might be better for you to hear it from me."

"It doesn't matter one way or the other."

Jenna could see it *did* matter. Blake had a past with Danielle Howard and her father, and Jenna wanted to know what it was.

"Thank your father for considering my reaction to his summons," Blake went on.

"It's not a summons, Blake," Danielle said impatiently. "And I wanted to do it because I thought…" She quickly glanced at Jenna. "I thought it would be good if we met face-to-face again and ironed everything out."

Obviously disturbed by the conversation, Blake studied Danielle pensively for a moment and then asked, "When's the meeting?"

"Eight o'clock tomorrow night at Dad's condominium in Sacramento."

"Fine. You and I can have a drink afterward if that's so important to you."

Jenna suspected the smile Danielle gave Blake was supposed to be sweet, sentimental, sultry and sexy all at the same time. It might have hit three of the four.

"It *is* important to me. Thank you. I'll see you then."

After Danielle walked away, Blake asked Jenna, "Are you in the mood for more music or do you want to go home?"

If they went home, she had the feeling Blake would lock himself in his den. "I'd like to stay a little while longer if that's okay with you."

"Fine," he said evenly, as if everything had changed between them.

Settled on the blanket once more, Jenna asked, "Is Danielle an old friend?"

"Danielle's not a friend." His voice was deep, and she realized his reply was only the tip of the iceberg.

"You haven't seen her for a while?"

He looked straight ahead at the band. "I haven't seen her in years."

As the steady beat pounded from the loudspeakers, Jenna couldn't contain the last important question. "Were you involved with her?"

Blake's body wasn't touching hers, and she could feel his emotional withdrawal as well. "I don't want to talk about it, Jenna."

"You're seeing her tomorrow night," she responded, not wanting to sound jealous, but feeling that way after all.

"It's not a date, and it has nothing to do with you."

Jenna didn't believe that for one minute. His meeting with Danielle Howard tomorrow night could have everything to do with her future. She felt his connection to the woman...and guessed something was unfinished between them.

The meeting with Nolan's backers had gone better than Blake expected. Preston Howard had kept his distance and stared at Blake often, as if trying to figure out how he could possibly be in the position he was now—with enough money to back a political candidate.

Blake took a swallow of the Scotch the maid had provided after he'd been shown to the study for his tête-à-tête with Danielle.

The door opened and she came into the room. She was wearing a low-cut black jumpsuit. He realized almost instantly his pulse was steady, not racing as it did when Jenna entered a room.

"Dad said your meeting went well," Danielle said with a smile. "Can I freshen your drink?" She moved to the bar to pour one of her own.

"I've got to get home. This is fine."

"To your pregnant wife?"

"Yes, to my pregnant wife."

Abandoning the bar and an idea of a drink, Danielle came to stand very close to him. "I called an old friend of mine who lives in Fawn Grove. She knows who Jenna is—the daughter of a minister. Has your taste in women changed so much?"

"I've changed a lot since we knew each other." Suddenly he realized he didn't care what Danielle thought. She *was* just a memory from his past who didn't matter anymore. What he wanted from Jenna was so very different from anything he'd ever wanted from Danielle. He really *had* changed.

Taking another tack, she said, "I really am sorry about your father, Blake. I hope you don't blame me."

Everything was always about Danielle. At least it had been. But not anymore. "I blame myself."

"Oh, Blake—"

"Danielle, I don't think a trip down memory lane will be good for either of us. We've both moved on. At least, I have."

"And you're very happy with your pregnant wife?"

It seemed she leaned a little closer and he wasn't tempted at all. "We're expecting our baby on August 21. I can't wait."

"If you ever need to get away from diapers and rattles and—"

Stepping back, he shook his head. "I've found someone to spend my life with, Danielle. You should do the same. Take care of yourself." He set down his drink on the bar and moved toward the door.

"Blake?"

He stopped.

"I wish I had married you that night."

"But you didn't. We'll never know how everything would have turned out if you had. I look forward now, not back."

Then he left Preston Howard's study, terrifically unsettled. He was no longer attracted to Danielle. He was beginning to feel as if Jenna filled his world. But he didn't fill hers. B.J. Winton did. Blake still wasn't sure how he was going to handle *that*.

It was almost midnight on Sunday when Jenna heard Blake come up the stairs. She told herself she should act nonchalant about his meeting with Danielle, but the way Blake was acting didn't make nonchalance possible. After his confrontation with Danielle, he'd been distant…unreachable. When they'd returned home from the carnival, he'd gone to his office and she'd spent the rest of the evening alone. She hadn't fallen asleep until almost 1:00 a.m., and he hadn't come up to his suite by then.

Now when she opened her bedroom door, he'd just reached the landing. Seeing her, he frowned. "Can't sleep?"

"No. I thought a glass of milk might help. How was your meeting?"

He came over to her door. "Is that why you couldn't sleep?"

"No, not exactly."

A few pulses of silence passed and then he admitted, "It's the first time I've ever been on equal terms with Preston Howard. I think he was unnerved by it."

She hadn't been referring to *that* meeting, but she was interested in Blake's connection to Danielle's father. "The two of you didn't get along?"

Blake laughed bitterly. "Get along? He had me arrested for kidnapping."

A small gasp snuck out before she could catch it. "Kidnapping?"

"No, you didn't marry a criminal, Jenna. Danielle and I were going to elope. We took off on my bike and Howard sent the police after us, saying I kidnapped her. With his influence, he probably could have made the charges stick."

"Not if she told the truth."

"Danielle was rebellious and defiant, but where her father was concerned, she always toed the line."

The way Blake was looking at her, Jenna wondered

if he thought that was true of *her,* too. "So *were* you charged?" she asked.

"Howard bargained with both me and Danielle—or blackmailed us—however you want to look at it. He told Danielle if she continued to see me, if she ever went through with the elopement, he'd cut off her allowance and refuse to pay her tuition to Berkeley, where she'd always dreamed of going. It took her all of a minute to choose. After one of those soulful looks at me, she stood by her father and swore she'd never see me again. Then, as if he wanted the added security that she wouldn't vacillate, he made a deal with me. He'd drop the charges if I agreed never to go near her again."

"And you agreed?"

"I agreed because I realized what I felt for Danielle had been a lot stronger than what she'd felt for me. She defected because of the nifty sports car her daddy promised her for graduation...because her friends were going to Berkeley, too...because she couldn't do without her father's allowance. Heaven forbid she should be independent and get a job."

Jenna heard not only the bitterness but what was underneath it. "You must have been terribly hurt."

His voice was rough. "I felt betrayed. I should have known better than to think—" His words came to an abrupt halt. Finally he went on, "After my mother died, I saw how loving someone had destroyed my father. He'd needed her too much. The way I felt that night at the police station... I've never forgotten it, and I never want to feel it again."

Now Blake's actions and reactions made perfect sense to her. "That's why you never married?"

"That's why. I don't believe in love, Jenna. I don't

believe in the theory of soul mates. People pair up for their own selfish reasons. We're a good example of that."

That statement shocked her. He must have seen that shock on her face because he asked, "Had you sugar-coated it? Decided it was noble to marry me for the sake of our child? Or did you actually marry me for access to your child and security? Marriages aren't made in heaven. They're made on earth for practical reasons."

She wanted to tell him he was wrong. She wanted to tell him marriage was so much more than that. She wanted to ask him about his father's suicide and what Danielle still meant to him. But she knew he wasn't in the mood to answer personal questions. Danielle's reappearance in his life had apparently stirred up bitterness and resentment and anger, and that was all he could see right now. Maybe it had been stirred up because he was still in love with Danielle Howard. She was divorced, but *he* was tied up. Did he regret their marriage?

Before she could figure out how to ask him that at least, Blake abruptly turned away. "I'm going to change and then work in my office downstairs." He was almost to his room when he said, "If you want a glass of milk, I'll bring it up."

She hurt when she thought about him still loving Danielle Howard. Did she hurt because it was a blow to her pride, or did she hurt for some other reason? "I think I'll skip the milk and read for a while."

He nodded. "See you tomorrow." Then he disappeared into his suite.

It suddenly dawned on Jenna that he'd told her nothing about his meeting with Danielle. Pictures of a beautiful blonde in Blake's arms played through her head and she knew no glass of milk, no amount of reading, no amount of sleep would banish them.

Just what would?

Chapter Ten

When Jenna looked back over her life, she didn't feel as if she'd made many wrong decisions. Yet for the past few weeks, she hadn't known whether her decisions were solid or built on sand. Today was a perfect example. She'd invited her father and brother to dinner. According to her father, Sunday was family day, and she'd reminded him of that this morning after church. That's when he'd reluctantly accepted her invitation.

For the past week, she and Blake had kept a cautious distance from each other. When she'd asked if he wanted to accompany her to her father's service, he'd declined. Yet when she told him about her plans for the evening, he assured her he'd be home by six, even if he hadn't finished eighteen holes on the golf course with Al. She was just glad his golf date included his right-hand man rather than Danielle Howard. She'd so badly wanted to ask if he'd been in touch with his first love since Sunday. But she didn't want to sound like a jealous wife. She didn't want to add force to the already turbulent waters swirling around them.

As she bustled around the kitchen with Marilyn, making sure everything was perfect for dinner, the doorbell rang. She froze. It was after six and Blake wasn't home. Already the evening was starting out on the wrong foot.

"I'll get that," Marilyn said as she dried her hands on a dish towel.

"No, I'll get it," Jenna assured her quickly. She wanted to welcome her father and Gary into the house herself.

When she opened the door, her father looked uncomfortable, though he was dressed casually in a short-sleeved, plaid, button-down shirt and cotton twill trousers.

Her brother wore his usual jeans, but his T-shirt was clean. He grinned at her. "I told Dad this was one cool place."

"Winston's done a good job of refurbishing it," her father admitted grudgingly. "It was run-down before he bought it."

She was glad they were beginning the evening on a positive note. "Come on in," she invited eagerly. "You can take a look around before we eat."

As her brother and father entered the foyer, Gary suggested, "Blake and I can show Dad the Mustang. It might bring back memories since he was around back then."

"Your mother liked Mustangs," Charles said with a wry smile. "But I wasn't the sports car type. It was lucky for me she adapted to a sedan."

Her father didn't talk about her mother much. Jenna

always wondered if it was too painful for him or if he'd forgotten his life with her. Now she could understand the difficulty in holding on, yet wanting to go forward. "I'm sure Blake would love to show you the car. He's…he's not here yet, but I'm certain he'll be here soon."

"He's working today?" her father asked.

"No, he's playing golf with a friend."

"I see."

Her father's tone told her he didn't expect to be welcomed by Blake.

To put their feet firmly on different ground, Jenna said, "I helped Marilyn make your favorite meal, Dad—pot roast, mashed potatoes and cherry pie."

"Marilyn?"

"Blake's housekeeper. You'll like her. She's as efficient as Shirley, but a lot more outspoken."

It was almost six-thirty when they sat down to dinner and Blake still hadn't arrived. Ten minutes later, Jenna heard the front door open. She'd been telling herself not to jump to conclusions. She'd hoped she could count on Blake, but tonight had given her reason to doubt that.

When he entered the dining room, he assessed the situation in a glance. "An accident on the freeway," he explained. "Al drove, and he doesn't have a car phone. I forgot my cell."

"It happens to the best of us," she said brightly, feeling so relieved she was giddy. Though there was tension between her and Blake, she didn't think he'd purposely avoid this dinner with her family. Yet she still wasn't sure of anything about him.

"We just started," she assured him. "I was telling Dad about our parenting class on Thursday night."

As Blake took a seat at the end of the table opposite her father, Charles commented, "Jenna tells me the class was about preparing homemade baby food. Think you'll give her a hand with that?"

Blake glanced at Jenna, then helped himself to the pot roast. "I'll do whatever needs to be done."

"Including changing diapers in the middle of the night?" her father asked.

Holding her breath, Jenna didn't know how much patience Blake would have with the probing.

"Jenna knows she can count on me to help her." After he served himself a helping of potatoes, he changed the subject and addressed Gary. "I've been talking to a friend in L.A. about your interest in film-making. Have you ever heard of Peter Selanki?"

"Selanki? The director of those documentaries that won so many awards?" Gary sounded awed.

Blake smiled. "He's the one. He's giving a weekend seminar in L.A. in three weeks—hands-on. Attendees have to bring camcorders and be ready to work. I got you a slot if you want it."

"You're kidding!"

"Wait a minute," Jenna's father said quickly. "A seminar like that will cost an arm and a leg. If you want to make those repairs to your car—"

Gary's face fell.

"Selanki gives three scholarships with each seminar. Do you have film you can submit to him along with an essay on why you want to be a director?"

"Sure! I can write the essay tonight and get it to you tomorrow."

"That's great. I'll overnight it to him."

Although Jenna's heart swelled with all of her newfound feelings for Blake, she could see her father wasn't happy.

"He needs my consent to go."

"Are you going to deny your son this once-in-a-lifetime opportunity?" Blake asked bluntly.

Evidently her dad wasn't cowed. "*You* look at it as an opportunity. I see it as a wasted weekend. Gary needs to set his sights on a reliable career, not one made of dreams and celluloid. You should have checked with me before you planned all this."

Already Jenna could feel Blake withdrawing and wanted to prevent it. Besides, this would be a chance for Gary to explore the career he thought he wanted. "It will be a wonderful experience for Gary, Dad—not just a seminar. He can spend time with other kids interested in the same thing he is."

"You think I'm going to let a seventeen-year-old go to L.A. and stay in a hotel with a crowd I don't know?"

"What if Jenna and I take Gary and spend the weekend there, too? We'll keep in contact with him when he's not in workshops and filming."

Her father didn't look much happier with that suggestion. "Jenna's more than seven months pregnant. It's too long a trip for her."

"Not if we stop often," she assured her father. "I can check with Dr. Palmer when I see him next week. Gary's been working all summer without a break," she reminded her dad. "The weekend will be good for him. And I haven't been to L.A. in a couple of years. It will be fun for all of us."

"If for some reason Jenna's doctor thinks she shouldn't go, I'll accompany Gary myself," Blake added.

Her father studied the food on his plate for a few moments, then looked at Blake and back at Jenna. "All right," he conceded grudgingly. "But I expect you to know where he is and what he's doing."

"We will." Jenna knew Gary would agree to being monitored in order to do this. If her father didn't give in once in a while, one of these days her brother was going to rebel big-time. Now Gary's smile of thanks let her know her bond with him was solid, even if the other bonds in her life right now were unsteady.

After dinner, they all sat in the living room and made stilted conversation until Gary suggested he and Blake show his father Blake's Mustang. Insisting he had work back at the parsonage to finish, Jenna's father told her he and Gary would leave afterward.

As she stood at the front window, Jenna watched the three of them enter the garage. Wandering into the kitchen, she went to the refrigerator for a glass of milk. She hadn't eaten much at dinner. She'd been too busy trying to keep the conversation rolling.

She'd just finished the milk when Blake came in the back door.

His expression was somber. "They're gone."

After she set her glass in the sink, she admitted, "I'm not sure dinner was a success or a failure. It's hard to tell with Dad sometimes."

"At least he came. But he's never going to approve of me."

She heard an odd note in Blake's voice. "Does it matter if he approves? It won't make any difference to us."

"You don't believe that, Jenna. Your father's disapproval is just another wedge—like B.J. He associates me with a fast life he doesn't want you to have any part of. But I don't know how to change the way I live, and I don't know if I want to. Not for him and not for you.''

She could see Blake was filled with frustration and she wanted to get to the root of it. ''I haven't asked you to change your life. But it *will* change once this baby's born.''

His gaze caught and held hers. ''I'm not talking about the baby and getting up in the middle of the night to change diapers, spending more time around here to be with a child. I'm talking about who I am, what I want and where I came from.''

Troubled by the intensity she saw in his eyes, she moved closer to him. ''What's bothering you so?''

The kitchen clock ticked until finally Blake answered. ''Danielle Howard's father disapproved of me as thoroughly as your father. I didn't have two nickels to rub together then. After my mom died and my father lost his job, we were on welfare and lived in a tenement. Howard saw me as a poor risk for his daughter.''

''He was a fool for not being able to see you wanted to make something of yourself.''

Blake's shrug was supposed to be offhand. ''Maybe. Maybe I didn't care so much about making something of myself until that night he almost had me arrested. I don't know. I think I always wanted the admiration and respect my father never earned. So I set out to get it along with enough money to make him comfortable.''

''How did you do that?'' she asked softly, sensing now was the time for this…now was the time for Blake to share who he was.

Going over to the window, Blake peered out over the gardens, as if looking out there helped the telling. ''I apprenticed with an electrician and had another job

at night. I worked twenty hours a day, learned everything I could, eventually hired on with a security firm.''

He stopped for so long she didn't know if he was
going to continue. But then he did. ''I called my father.
I wrote to him. But I didn't get back here. I couldn't
return to this town until I'd found some measure of
success. I'd finally saved up enough money to get my
own company started when my dad committed suicide.''

''Blake, I'm sorry.''

At her sincere empathy, he faced her again. ''If I
had stayed in Fawn Grove and not gone to L.A. when
I was eighteen, my being here might have prevented
my dad from taking his life. He needed money, just
like everyone needs money. But he needed me more.
When I left, I think I took the last of the meaning of
his life with me.''

She shook her head. ''You can't blame yourself for
what he did. Your staying might not have prevented
anything. And where would you be now?''

Blake didn't answer her question. Rather, he was
looking at her curiously. ''You don't seem surprised
by what I just told you.''

''My father told me about your dad,'' she confessed.
''I wanted to bring it up several times, but didn't know
how.''

His hands tightened by his sides. ''Am I so unapproachable, Jenna?''

She didn't know how to explain the mixture of desire
and excitement, anxiety and guilt that plagued her
whenever he came within two feet of her. ''You're not
unapproachable. But that information was so personal....''

"Yet your father felt the need to share it. And probably right after he met me. I wonder why. Maybe he wanted to imply I might take after my father and that might make you not want to get involved with me."

She felt herself blush because that had been her dad's intent.

"You didn't know me at all, Jenna. Did you want security for you and your child so much you were willing to ignore that possibility?"

When she didn't respond right away, he snapped, "Never mind. Just so you know, I've never had a suicidal thought. Not even the night I thought I might be arrested for kidnapping. I'm a survivor, Jenna, and I'm going to teach our child to be one, too." Stepping away from her, he said, "I'll be in my office the rest of the night working on the security for Evanston's event."

Before she could assure Blake that from the moment she'd met him she'd realized he was not only a survivor but a fighter, too, he left the kitchen. When her father had told her about Blake's father's suicide, she'd already known somehow that Blake had been cast in a different mold than his father. Her husband's life fire burned too brightly to have it flicker because of despair. Maybe later she could tell him. Maybe later she could thank him for the opportunity he'd found for Gary.

Thinking about Blake's question about approachability, she realized he wasn't unapproachable, but the tension between them made approaching him a risk. She wasn't used to taking risks. If she wanted her marriage to work, she might have to learn how to jump without a parachute.

* * *

On Tuesday evening, Blake stood outside the pas-senger side of the senator's limousine, his portable ra-dio ready as he listened for Al's all-clear sign.

In spite of himself, he thought about Jenna. He'd hardly seen her since Sunday. After he'd picked up Gary's package for Peter yesterday, he'd overnighted it from his office in Sacramento and worked late in preparation for tonight. This morning he'd been out of the house by 6:00 a.m. Once again he considered his conversation with her on Sunday—the fact she'd known about his father and married him, anyway. Had she truly not been worried he was anything like his dad? Had they connected on that deep a level? Or had financial security been her motivating factor for mar-rying him?

Suddenly Al's voice pierced the chatter and hubbub around him. "Ready if you are. Are you sure you don't want me to stand in for John?"

Focusing on the job at hand, Blake thought about Al's suggestion. John Varstead, a former bouncer, had gotten food poisoning last night and was in no condi-tion to protect anyone. Blake had decided to do the job himself to make sure it was done right. "We'll go ahead as planned. All entrances are secure. Everyone was screened by the metal detector?"

"We used the wand on everyone" came Al's reply. "There's nothing more we can do except pat down each guest, and I don't think these people would go for it."

"We'll keep Evanston surrounded," Blake returned. "Mark is on the security cameras and he knows exactly what to look for."

"Let's move him in, then," Al decided, and clicked off.

When Blake opened the door of the limo, he nodded

to the senator. Evanston climbed out and straightened his tie, then his suit jacket.

Blake had given James Evanston instructions, and he wanted to make sure he'd been clear. "Don't make a move without us moving with you."

As two of the guards closed ranks with Blake, Evanston replied, "I've had threats before and they've come to nothing. I'm not going to let them change how I relate to my constituents."

"Tonight you're *my* responsibility. Don't step out of the route we planned. Don't do anything impulsive. Got it?"

"Got it," Evanston murmured, more concerned with the wrinkle in his suit jacket.

There were four men close to Evanston, including Blake. Two others unobtrusively flanked them. After Blake signaled his men, they moved forward in concert almost mechanically, having done this a hundred times before.

A path had been cleared for them and roped off. Blake tried to see everyone and see everywhere as they entered the hotel. All of Evanston's supporters were seated inside the ballroom at tables for eight. Blake had completed background checks on every one of them. He knew if the evening proceeded smoothly, Evanston's guard would be down and that meant Blake had to be more alert.

Blake scanned the lobby. Unfortunately they couldn't close the hotel to other guests. There were two couples at the reception desk checking in, a man in a navy suit with a geometrically patterned tie standing at the concierge's desk. Two women sat conversing on one of the leather couches. Nothing to alert him to danger.

They kept moving across the marble floor of the large lobby.

Then suddenly, Blake's intuition told him there'd been a shift. Evanston smiled and waved to a woman in a red dress immediately inside the ballroom. A waiter with a water pitcher—Blake recognized his face from one of the background checks—moved around one of the tables. No one could get into this ballroom without an engraved pass. No one could get near the senator....

There was an unexpected rush of movement, and Blake instinctively stepped in front of Evanston. He shouted for Evanston to get down, but the senator didn't move and Blake blocked him with his body. He saw the flash of a geometrically patterned tie as a sharp pain seared his arm and then his side. He wasn't concerned with that. His body had to protect the senator's, had to shield it, had to ward off anything that would hurt the man.

Yet as Blake finally forced Evanston down and covered the senator with his body, Jenna's face flashed in front of his eyes. He blinked to dismiss it now when all his faculties had to be geared to what was happening—the shouts, Al's voice on the radio, policemen hurrying toward them. Still he couldn't clear Jenna's face from his vision. Her eyes were always so tender, so velvety-brown whenever she talked about their baby.

A shot rang out and Blake felt weaker as his ears buzzed. The pain in his arm and his side became numbingly cold as he realized he might not live to see the birth of his child.

When Marilyn rushed into the porch, she cried, "Come quick, Mrs. Winston. I think Mr. Winston's been hurt. It's on TV."

The horrified look on Marilyn's face sunk in before her words did. Then her news galvanized Jenna. Pushing herself out of the chair, she hurried after Marilyn into the living room.

The TV was blaring and a local anchor was describing the scene. "Senator James Evanston was the target, but Blake Winston, the CEO of the security firm guarding Senator Evanston, was taken to Mercy General Hospital along with the attacker, who was shot by police and taken into custody. No one has given us a report yet on the extent of their injuries. The attacker, a man pretending to be a hotel patron, went after the senator with an ivory letter opener. He was in the vicinity as the senator and his security force made their way into the ballroom. Blake Winston, who usually stays in the background overseeing this type of operation, had stepped in for his bodyguard, John Varstead, who'd apparently taken ill with food poisoning last night."

"I have to get to the hospital." Jenna turned away from the TV.

"You shouldn't drive yourself, ma'am. Mr. Winston wouldn't want you driving while you're upset. We can take my car—"

"No. You have to stay here in case there's any word. You can call me on my cell phone. I'll try to get hold of my father on the way. If he should call, or Gary, tell them what happened."

"I still think you shouldn't be going alone."

Getting hold of herself, Jenna took Marilyn's hand and reassured her. "During the past two years, I saw my late husband through countless chemo treatments.

I sat by his bed and watched him die. I made the decision to have this baby after he died and I married Blake because——'' She stopped and took a breath. ''I've been more on my own in the past two years than in my whole life. I'll be fine, Marilyn. Trust me. I'm just pregnant. I'm not going to break, fold or faint. I'll call you when I know something.''

Then, not knowing if she had the time to give Marilyn any more reassurance, she grabbed her purse and rushed out the door.

She was backing her car out of the garage when Marilyn ran up to it and signaled for her to roll down the window.

''What is it?'' Jenna asked impatiently.

''Mr. Winston called. He's coming home. Said he's fine, and he'll be here as fast as Al can drive him back.''

First she felt inordinate relief. Then worry plagued her again as she wondered if Blake really was fine or if that was just his interpretation. ''Did he say anything about his injuries?''

''No, ma'am. But if the doctor let him go, it can't be too bad, can it?''

''I sincerely hope not. I just know how determined Blake can be, and if he didn't want to stay in that hospital, nothing would keep him there.''

Marilyn gave an understanding nod. ''I'm going to make a chicken casserole I know will go down easy. Is there anything else you think I should do?''

''You start on that, and I'll put the car back in the garage.'' She knew she had to keep busy. ''I'll make a pitcher of that herbal tea I bought. Blake had a glass earlier in the week and said he liked it. We're not going to know what we need to do for him until he gets here.''

It was almost an hour later until Al and Blake came into the house. In spite of Marilyn's protest, Jenna had made peach custards, too, and was waiting until they came out of the oven. She knew she'd drive herself crazy if she sat alone somewhere. She'd called the parsonage, but no one had answered and she'd left a message.

Now as she hurried to the foyer, she saw Blake and froze. His complexion was ashen. His white dress shirt, minus a tie and opened at the throat, was stained with blood from his armpit to his waist. There was also an irregular circle of red on his sleeve.

''I knew I should have thrown this damn shirt away at the hospital and come home without it. It's not as bad as it looks, Jenna,'' Blake adamantly insisted.

Al quickly jumped in. ''The doctor said he's going to be fine. He would have preferred if Blake stayed overnight....''

Blake shot Al a look that should have knocked him flat.

''Why didn't you stay?'' Jenna asked, her voice shaky as she approached him.

''Because I'll be more comfortable here. No one can get any sleep in a hospital. Besides that, I don't belong there.''

Instead of asking Blake, she turned to Al. ''How serious was it?''

He must have been able to tell by her tone that she wanted the truth and all of it. Obviously torn by loyalty to his boss as well as a code of honor that wouldn't let him lie to a pregnant lady, he was slow to answer. Finally he gave a what-can-I-do look to Blake and replied, "He had a three-inch gash in his side—not too deep—and one in his arm. The doc stitched him up and he's pretty numb now. He'll be feeling a lot worse in a couple of hours."

"If you weren't so good at your job, I'd fire you." Blake's expression was angry.

"You can't fire Al for telling me what I need to know," Jenna maintained calmly. "I would have called the doctor if he hadn't told me. Do you need help to go up to your room?"

Blake moved slowly toward the living room. "I'm not going up to my room. I'll be perfectly comfortable watching TV."

"You should be in bed! What if in a couple of hours you *do* feel bad and I can't get you up the steps?"

"You can call me, ma'am," Al said chivalrously, as if he knew she wasn't going to win this argument.

Stopping just outside the living room, Blake scowled. "*You* live in Sacramento. I'm not going to bring you back here. If you just get me some comfortable clothes from my bedroom—"

"I'll get them," Jenna said quickly, needing something to do.

"Jenna…" Blake warned.

"I'm not the one who was stabbed. You are. Those steps are good exercise for me. Just tell me where your clothes are."

If Al thought this conversation was unusual between a husband and wife, he didn't give any indication.

Seeing that Jenna would fight him on this, Blake gave in. "T-shirts are in the third chest drawer, shorts are in the bottom drawer." He turned to Al. "Thanks for bringing me home. If the doctor hadn't given me that shot, I'd have driven myself."

"You shouldn't have driven, anyway," Al said with a shake of his head. Leaning close to Blake, he whispered in an undertone, "If she wants to take care of you, let her. That's what women do best."

Blake just frowned. "I don't need anyone to take care of me. I'm going to watch TV for a while, then get a good night's sleep."

Al took a pharmacy bag from his pocket and handed it to Blake. "Follow the directions and don't leap any tall buildings in a single bound if you can help it. At least not for twenty-four hours." His tone was measured, exasperated, and laced with what both men would deny was affection.

Addressing Jenna, Al smiled. "I'd stay and help, but he'll blow a gasket if I do." He took a card from his pocket and handed it to her. "Call me if he gives you any trouble. I have a feeling he'll be better behaved for you than for me."

After he walked to the door, he stopped when he reached for the knob. "You saved Evanston's life, Blake. You saw it coming and prevented it from happening. So don't fault yourself because you didn't nab the creep sooner. Got it?"

Silent for a few moments, Blake finally nodded. "Got it."

There was silence again as Al left and closed the door.

Jenna asked softly, "Are you sure you don't want to go upstairs?"

Blake's gray eyes locked with hers. "Positive."

"Then I'll be right back," she told him as she headed for the stairs. On the first step, she tossed over her shoulder, "When I come down, I want to know exactly what happened."

Chapter Eleven

When Jenna entered the living room, Blake was sitting on the couch, his shirt in a ball next to his feet. He had his legs stretched out in front of him, and his head rested on the back of the sofa. She suspected he was feeling a lot worse now than he had in the adrenaline rush and shock of everything that had happened. Yet knowing Blake, he wouldn't admit it.

Hearing her footsteps, he sat up.

After she laid his clothes on the sofa next to him, she scooped up the soiled shirt. ''I think we'll just toss this into the trash.''

''It's probably a good idea. I don't need any reminders of what happened today.''

Taking advantage of him bringing up the subject, she sat beside him. ''Al said there was nothing else you could have done.''

''I should have sensed the guy coming a split second

sooner. I should have had men behind the desk listen-
ing. I should have—''

"Should have, what if, if only. You're old enough
to know they don't do much good.''

He was silent for a few long moments. ''No, I'm
not. I always go back over what I could have done
better.''

"Ah, a perfectionist,'' she said, with an attempt to
lighten his mood.

"In the work I do, everything *does* have to be perfect. If that man had gotten to Evanston, it would have
been *my* fault.''

She knew there was no point in arguing with him
on that. ''But he didn't get to Evanston...*because* of
you. I heard on the news he used an ivory letter
opener.''

"As sharp as a knife blade,'' Blake muttered. ''I
don't know if we even would have found it if we'd
patted him down. This work is getting harder and
harder, Jenna.''

"After today, I'll worry every time you go out. I
never thought you'd be on the front line.'' When she'd
heard the news, she'd felt panicked and terrified. Looking at Blake now—with disheveled hair, his pained
gray eyes, his bare chest—she realized her world would
stop if anything happened to him. She...

She loved Blake Winston!

The realization was so heart-stoppingly sudden it
made her catch her breath.

Apparently he noticed, and he swiftly covered her
hand with his. ''I'm not usually in danger. You can't
worry every time I go out on a job.'' Then, attempting
a smile, he quipped, ''You'll have gray hair before our
son or daughter is five.''

Jenna tried to respond to his humor with a weak smile. She couldn't sit here so close to him, couldn't breathe in the same air he did, couldn't wish his arms were around her...until she absorbed the fact she loved him. Her world rocked with it because she'd thought she was still in love with B.J. She couldn't love two men, could she?

"You must be hungry. I'm going to see what's keeping Marilyn." Pulling her hand from under Blake's, she hurried out into the hall and just stood there, her hands on her tummy, her emotions in a whirl.

Hadn't she married Blake because she was attracted to him? Hadn't she married Blake because she'd felt drawn to him? Yes, it was all because of their baby, but she wouldn't have just married *any* man.

Confusion rippled through her as she realized the repercussions of all this. She loved Blake, but he'd said he didn't believe in love. He'd said he wanted a partnership.

Marilyn came into the hall and saw her. "Mrs. Winston, is everything all right? Mr. Winston shouldn't really be in the hospital, should he?"

Composing herself, Jenna shook her head. "I think we can take care of him as well as any nurses can, don't you?"

Marilyn grinned. "You bet we can. Let's see if we can't get him to eat something."

By the time Jenna and Marilyn returned to the living room, Blake had changed into jogging shorts. The T-shirt still lay folded on the sofa.

Every time Jenna looked at the hair on Blake's chest her insides went quivery.

Jenna was glad to see Marilyn fussing around the sofa, making sure his portion of chicken casserole was big enough. After he assured her everything was fine, she left.

Jenna couldn't seem to settle down. "Do you have medicine to take?"

He motioned to the bag on the coffee table. "After I've eaten. The antibiotic's all I need. I don't want to be numbed up and not know what's going on."

"Wouldn't it be better to get a good night's sleep…?" she began. But then the phone rang. "I'll get it," she told him so he wouldn't have to get up.

"Jenna," her father said in a rush. "I got your message and saw the clip on the news. Is Winston in the hospital?"

"No, he's here. The doctor let him come home. I'm not sure he should have, though."

She saw Blake frown at her words.

"How serious were his injuries?"

She explained what Al had told her.

"He saved Senator Evanston's life." Her father sounded surprised.

"Yes, he did. That's the kind of man Blake is," she added.

"Evanston is an important man and apparently it was Winston's job to protect him."

"I think it's more than a job to him, Dad, and that's what worries me. It could happen again."

"Has it happened before?"

She felt Blake's gaze on her. "I don't think so."

Her father must have heard the worry in her voice. "This is more than a marriage for the sake of your baby, isn't it."

"I can't talk about that now." The truth was, she was still trying to figure it out.

"If you need to talk, Jenna…"

"Can you listen with an open mind?"

The many ticks of silence told her her father was considering her question seriously. "I can try."

"Maybe sometime," she responded. "I've got to go now."

"Is he letting you take care of him?"

She knew her father was thinking of B.J., who'd been grateful for every little thing she'd done. "Barely," she replied, knowing Blake had an innate sense of pride that didn't want her to see weakness on his part. She had to convince him to let his guard down with her. If he didn't, he'd never be able to love her back.

"Keep me posted," her father said.

"I will."

"I'm glad he's all right, Jenna. You don't need any more chaos in your life right now."

She was pensive as she set down the phone and noticed Blake had eaten only a few forkfuls of his supper. His eyes were on her as she perched on the armchair a safe distance away from him. "Dad says he's glad you weren't hurt badly."

"He's thinking of you."

She couldn't deny that. "He doesn't wish you any harm."

"Maybe not, but I'm sure he wishes I were out of your life."

"That's not going to happen." She was thinking about more than the baby now.

"I don't want you to worry about me, Jenna. It's not good for you. Especially now."

It was more concern than worry, more fear than she could ever imagine. "I can't turn worry off and on very well."

"It's unfounded. This was just a fluke. Usually I supervise. That's all."

"No, usually you run the operation. And if you saw someone who was in danger again, you'd be there, protecting him."

Shaking his head, he insisted, "Forget all that stuff Al said. I don't think I'm Superman."

That gave her just the lead-in she needed. "Good, then you won't mind admitting you should go to bed early and let your body heal."

"I walked right into that, didn't I?" he asked with a wry smile. When he lifted the tray to set it on the coffee table, he winced, then quickly covered the pain.

"I'm going to go upstairs with you and make sure you get settled." She intended to do whatever she had to for him to feel more comfortable and heal quickly.

"I don't need a baby-sitter, Jenna."

Although she was confused about the newfound love she'd realized for Blake and what it would mean to her life, she insisted, "I'm your wife. Let me take care of you."

"Because it's your duty?" His gray eyes were piercing.

"Because I want you to get better as soon as you can. Fighting me, fighting rest, fighting the medicine isn't going to help you."

He drove his fingers through his hair and then pushed himself to his feet. "I have calls to make before I can even think about going to bed."

"Blake…"

This time his voice was weary as he asked, "Don't argue with me about it, okay?"

She offered a compromise. "Can you make them in here?"

"My files are in my office."

"If you tell me where to look, I'll get them for you."

Silence ticked by until he said, "You win."

After she brought him what he needed from his office, she left him alone on the pretense of putting away his tray. In the kitchen she made up a dish of snacks in case he awakened later and was hungry. After she poured more tea, she told Marilyn she'd take care of anything else he needed for the night. She knew if she waited and offered to help him up the stairs, he'd refuse. So instead, she went up to his suite, put the glass of tea, a glass of juice and the snack plate on his bedside table, then went to her bathroom for a quick shower. She intended to stay up here and make sure she was close by if he needed anything.

She'd just dried her hair and slipped on a nightgown and robe when she heard him coming up the stairs. She waited until he'd gone into his room and then she went to his door and pushed it open. He was prone on the bed, his hand on his side, and he looked as if he was in a lot of pain.

Crossing to the bed, she knelt down beside him. "Can I do anything?" she asked in a low voice.

"Yes. Don't tell me I'm crazy when I have a meeting here tomorrow morning on the Evanston matter."

She didn't even protest, because it wouldn't do any good. "At least you're not driving to Sacramento." Her tone was dry.

That brought a smile to his lips. "I'm not altogether stupid."

She so badly wanted to brush his hair over his brow, but she didn't feel the freedom to do that. "I'm glad to hear it," she teased, taking his hand in spite of herself.

His fingers squeezed hers. "I called my office for messages. Peter Selanki left one. He got your brother's material this morning and he looked it over. Gary's been accepted for the seminar weekend, and he got one of the scholarships."

"He'll be thrilled!" Then she realized that weekend was scheduled in two and a half weeks. "Will you be all right then? I mean, I can always go with him myself...."

"I'll be good as new. I want to show you my favorite spots. I'm more concerned about you traveling."

She'd spoken to her doctor about it this morning. "Dr. Palmer said I'll be fine—as long as we stop for me to stretch and take a bathroom break," she added with a grin.

"I'm going to lease a limo for the drive so you're comfortable and can move around. We'll stop whenever you say."

He was such a thoughtful man. Simply because she was carrying his child? Or was there more behind the nice things he did for her? If so, would he ever admit it?

His eyes drifted closed, and Jenna didn't know whether to stay or go. As if he could read her thoughts, he turned to look at her again. "There is something you could do for me tonight."

"What?"

"Sleep with me. I mean, sleep in my bed." Then, as if he realized what he'd requested, he let go of her hand and pulled back. "Never mind. That was all the drugs they gave me talking. I'll be fine."

She wasn't exactly sure why he'd made the request. *Was* it the drugs talking? Did Blake want to ease her into his bed slowly? Or did he just need the emotional comfort of another human being staying close? It didn't matter. He'd been kind and gentle and tender with her. And she loved him.

Rising to her feet, she went around his bed and climbed in the other side.

"Jenna..."

"I'll be right here in case you need anything."

"Are you sure?"

"If the baby kicks too much, or I keep you awake, I'll leave."

"You won't disturb me," he said in a husky voice, rolling onto his good side and facing her. Then he closed his eyes and she heard deep, even breaths.

Turning toward him, she pulled up the sheet and watched him sleep.

When Jenna awakened, she almost felt as if she were still dreaming. But the reality of Blake's chest hair under her fingers, her chin tucked above his shoulder as she shared his king-size pillow, reminded her she wasn't dreaming. After she'd turned out the light, she'd intended to stay on her side of the bed. What had happened?

Her concern and blossoming love for Blake had happened. That love still didn't feel quite right. Because she didn't know if Blake would ever love her? Because she was still attached to B.J. and memories of their life together?

She'd married a stranger, stood up to her father and been propelled into a life she'd never expected. Now she was curled up beside Blake as if he were truly her husband—

"Are you awake?" His deep, sandy voice startled

her. When she went to move away, he said, "I like you there."

But she felt embarrassed. "I...guess I rolled over here in the middle of the night." Sliding away from him, she lay on her back and stared up at the ceiling, rather than into his knowing gray eyes. "How are you feeling?"

"Like a truck ran over me. But I have to get ready for the meeting. They're coming at nine."

Looking at the bedside clock, she saw it was seven. "You have time."

"I have a feeling getting dressed this morning is going to take some time."

Raising herself on her elbows, she said, "I'll go see if Marilyn—"

"Jenna?" he asked, and there was note in his voice that made her look at him this time.

"What?"

"Can I feel the baby?"

It was a request any father would make. "Sure. He's moving around. You might really be able to feel him."

She lay perfectly still as Blake rolled on his side and moved closer to her. His hair-roughened thigh brushed against her hip as he lay his hand on her tummy. "Any place in particular?" he asked, almost tentatively.

"Just be still and you'll be able to feel everything."

Blake splayed his fingers. The heat of his palm scorched through the layer of cotton. Her robe had opened during the night and it now lay on either side of her. She should feel more shy about this. She should wonder if he could see through the material. All thoughts fled as she watched Blake's face and he felt their son or daughter move for the first time. "I felt

it!'' There was awe in Blake's voice and she understood it completely. ''There it goes again.''

''It's almost constant sometimes. I think we're going
to have a track star.''

Blake's gaze met hers and she felt something so deep
inside, it scared her.

His hand was still hot on her belly. ''I didn't think
you'd stay all night.''

''I told you I would. You didn't move much. Is that
because you were sleeping so soundly, or because you
were in pain?''

''Sleeping soundly. Knowing you were there beside
me, I was able to...relax.''

But his eyes were getting darker and she had the
feeling he wasn't relaxed now. ''Jenna...'' he began.

''I have to ask you something,'' she blurted out, sitting up.

His expression was patient. ''What?''

She didn't know how to word her question tactfully.
''When you and Danielle Howard had a drink, did old
feelings crop up?''

The nerve in his jaw worked as he hiked himself up
to a sitting position. ''I told you before, Danielle has
nothing to do with us.''

''She does if anything happened when you saw her.
You didn't get home till 2:00 a.m. that night.''

When Blake didn't answer but studied Jenna with a
scrutiny he'd never employed before, she felt as if she
were trying to obtain high-level security clearance.

There was restrained tension in Blake. All the uncertainty that plagued their marriage was a wall between them as he answered, ''My meeting with Preston
Howard lasted until almost one. I spent a short time
with Danielle. But I don't think that's really what you

want to know. I told you once before, if I married you, I wouldn't be unfaithful.''

"You also said you wouldn't live like a monk."

"You don't trust me, do you, Jenna? Besides your own doubts, your father has piled on a few more. Did you trust Winton after you'd dated him a few weeks?"

"That was different. He didn't have…your reputation or a woman in the wings who had a look in her eye that meant she was still interested."

"Are you jealous?" he asked seriously.

"No!" she answered too quickly. "But if we…if we—"

"Have sex," he said dryly.

"If we make love," she corrected him, "I have to know you're committed to our marriage."

Now, in spite of his injuries, he moved quickly and got out of bed. "I think I've proved I'm committed to this baby."

"Yes, to the baby—but not necessarily to our marriage."

He shook his head. "Just what do you want?"

She realized now how much she wanted his love. She needed the security of that before she'd truly be his wife. But she didn't know how to tell him that, and she wasn't going to beg for something he couldn't give.

When she couldn't seem to answer him, he went to his closet and pulled a shirt from a hanger. "Danielle Howard is no more a fly in the ointment than B.J. Winton is."

"B.J.'s gone," she protested, reminding herself for the umpteenth time.

"Gone, but not forgotten. You're still heartbroken about it. What kind of marriage can we have if you won't let go of the past?"

She couldn't deny she still loved B.J., just as she couldn't deny that she still missed him. Her new love for Blake was so fresh, so precarious, she couldn't express it. She couldn't take the risk of telling him she loved him when she didn't know how much he cared for her. Sex was one thing, love was another matter entirely. More than seven months pregnant now, she felt ungainly.

When she climbed out of Blake's bed, she said, "I think we both know letting go of the past isn't so simple."

"It could be as simple as making a decision about it," he said practically.

"Everything B.J. and I shared is part of who I am, just as everything you and Danielle shared—"

He cut her off. "An eighteen-year-old with raging hormones doesn't know a lot about sharing. Yes, I have memories of Danielle. But she doesn't have to be part of the future if I don't want her to be. Can you say the same thing about your dead husband?"

Apparently that was the whole problem. She didn't think of B.J. as dead.

Blake moved toward his bathroom. "I have to get ready for my meeting."

"If you need any help..." Her voice trailed off, as she knew he wouldn't accept help from her right now.

"I'm capable of getting dressed myself, Jenna. I'll buzz Marilyn after everyone's here so she can serve coffee. If you have plans for today, don't change them. I'll be tied up until afternoon."

He was telling her he didn't need her in his life. He was telling her he was in control...again.

"I'm going to run a few errands—for the baby. I'll have my cell phone if you need me."

First on her list was a visit to B.J.'s parents to tell them she'd married Blake. She wasn't looking forward to it. Considering the discussion she and Blake just had, she couldn't tell him about *that* errand.

After he stepped into the bathroom, he faced her again. "Don't put everything you buy away. I'd like to see it when I'm finished with my meetings." Then he closed his bathroom door.

She left Blake's room certain of one thing—he *was* committed to his child. Was that enough to build on for their marriage to succeed?

Marilyn had helped Jenna carry her purchases up to the spare room that had been designated for the nursery. The only piece of furniture in the room was her mother's rocker. Blake had emptied the room, telling Jenna whenever she wanted to order furniture, she should. It was perfect for a baby with its sunny yellow walls. Today she'd found a puffed cotton wall hanging of a rainbow and clouds and children swinging in a balloon basket.

She'd needed to think about the baby after her visit to B.J.'s parents. It hadn't been any easier than the last time she'd stopped in and told them her child would not be their grandchild. They'd been shocked then but hadn't blamed Jenna for the mistake. Today, however, she'd seen the recriminations in their eyes when she'd told them she'd married Blake. They'd wished her well but didn't try to hide concern that she was making a mistake.

Before she'd left, Charlene Winton had taken her aside and said, "I understand why you married him, Jenna, but I wish you'd given B.J.'s memory a little more time and respect. You could have had this child and married later.''

Why hadn't she waited? Why had she let Blake convince her to marry him now? Maybe because from the very first meeting, they'd formed a bond. Maybe because she'd been more attracted to him than any man she'd ever met. How long did everyone expect her to grieve? It had been over a year and a half.

Yet she understood how much the Wintons missed B.J. She understood that they'd considered her a daughter and now that she'd married Blake, they'd lost her, too.

She had six weeks until her due date. Would her emotions be any more settled then?

Jenna crossed to the corner of the room where she and Marilyn had placed the packages, then lowered herself to the floor and began sorting through them. She wanted to wash the sleepers, playsuits and tiny stockings. She'd bought outfits in yellow, green, peach and combined pink and blue. She'd also bought pacifiers, bottles, a baby thermometer and a few packages of disposable diapers.

She'd spread everything around her in organized piles by the time Blake stopped in the doorway. He'd worn a button-down chambray shirt and navy slacks for his meeting. There were lines on his forehead and around his eyes, as if the day had taken its toll.

Entering the room, he eyed the baby clothes and necessities. ''It looks as if you made a good start. Marilyn said she helped you carry it all up. I would have taken care of that this evening.''

He would have, and it would have cost him.

''The packages were light. There were just a lot of them.''

Still feeling the tension between them from their discussion this morning, she scooped up a baby shirt and rose to her feet. Approaching him, she held it out. "Isn't this adorable?" Tiny cats and dogs danced all over the cotton.

Blake took it from her and it seemed very small in his large hand. When he checked the label, he saw it read Newborn. "What if our son or daughter weighs ten pounds? I heard babies are born larger now."

"Then I guess he or she will only wear it for a week or two. I bought a few in the three-month size and the six-month size, too."

He picked up a yellow blanket embroidered with two giraffes. "Are you going to bring the baby home from the hospital in this?"

"Probably." She picked up the little terry romper and hat that had giraffe patterns. "These go with it."

Blake smiled and shook his head. "I can see a trip through the baby department will be an adventure." There was amusement in his tone and an almost-smile on his lips.

"You said to buy what we needed, so I ordered furniture, too." She took a sheaf of paper out of the pocket of her jeans. "I have pictures. If you don't like it, I can call the store and cancel it."

Taking the flyer from her, he examined the walnut crib, changing table and chest. "It looks good to me. When can they deliver it?"

"Next week. I should be able to get the nursery set up before we go to L.A."

His dark gray eyes studied her carefully. "I don't want you lifting or climbing stepladders."

"I promise I won't."

"And if you need help, ask for it."

"I promise, I will."

He smiled at her then, as if he saw this as the step forward they needed. Maybe that's why she'd done it. Yet she could still hear Charlene Winton's voice in her ear. *I wish you'd given B.J.'s memory a little more time and respect.*

She had given B.J. all of her love and all of her respect, but now it was time she moved forward. Maybe it *was* as easy as making a decision.

Chapter Twelve

As Jenna, Blake and Gary crossed the lobby of the five-star hotel, Gary gave a low whistle. "I've never been in a place like this."

"Pete always goes all out for these seminars," Blake said with a smile. "I guess he wants to give you a taste of what it will be like if you *do* succeed."

As Jenna tried to soak in everything about the hotel—from its crystal chandelier to its contemporary sculpture on the dais in the middle of the lobby, she was grateful Blake had given her brother this opportunity. She was more than grateful Blake had recovered from his injuries so quickly. On the other hand, she knew his will was strong enough to make most anything happen. After the night he'd been hurt, she'd returned to sleeping in her own room. But this weekend...that could change.

The clerk at the desk knew Blake and smiled

warmly. After he checked the roster for Peter Selanki's seminars, he gave Gary the room number and the name of the young man he'd be rooming with.

Blake asked the seventeen-year-old, "Do you want us to go up with you or do you want to go up alone?"

Gary smiled sheepishly. "I'd rather go alone."

As if he understood, Blake nodded. "I'll call your room in about a half hour to see if you've hooked up with anyone. If not, we could go sightseeing."

Agreeing, Gary gave Jenna a wide grin and took off toward the elevator, eager to begin his weekend.

After Blake turned back to the desk, the clerk gave him a room packet with two keys. "There are two bedrooms in the suite as you requested."

Ever since Jenna had ordered the baby furniture, a new closeness existed between her and Blake. There was still a delicious tension snapping between them, but at times he seemed to relax with her now. Last night as they'd taken a walk around the gardens, he'd told her more about growing up in Fawn Grove and what it had been like after his mom died. His father had essentially stopped living. He'd gone to work, come home to drink and passed out in bed. After the loss of his job, he'd sat around the house all day in the dark, shades drawn. Jenna had been able to see easily why Blake had wanted to escape Fawn Grove, why he had wanted to become a success to change his father's life. He still carried around guilt concerning his dad's suicide, and she suspected he was afraid to love because that meant he was responsible for someone else's happiness. She wasn't a therapist, but it seemed logical to her. Along with Danielle's betrayal, no wonder he'd constructed walls that were hard to tear down.

Still…she'd felt as if they'd torn down a few of them over the past week.

When he gave her one of the keys, he simply said, "This seemed to be the most practical."

She took it, not responding. She didn't know how she felt about the two-bedroom suite—it was definitely cozier than separate rooms. But if Blake had reserved only one bedroom, she wouldn't have protested.

They took the elevator to the fifth floor and stepped inside. The suite was decorated in peach and aqua. The foyer led into a living room with a sofa, love seat and entertainment center, and a hall led to the bedrooms. The doorman had just brought in their luggage when the telephone rang.

When Jenna answered it, she heard Gary's excited voice. "Hey, sis. My roommate's here. We're going to hang out downstairs with some other guys. You and Blake do your thing."

"Do you want to go to dinner with us later?"

"Probably not. I think we'll all go get pizza at some famous place. I'll call you tonight when I get in so you know I'm safely tucked in my room."

After Jenna hung up the phone, she turned to Blake. "He's off and running. He said he'd call when he gets in tonight."

"There's a message service if we're not here," Blake explained as he carried her suitcase to her bedroom.

She followed him and asked, "Where will we be?"

"How about a night on the town? You haven't really lived until you've seen L.A. at night."

"I brought the outfit I wore for the party on your boat. Will that be appropriate?"

His gray eyes held the silver sparks she'd become

accustomed to—the ones that meant he was thinking about kissing her, the ones that meant he was thinking about more than a night on the town. ''That will be perfect.'' His gaze went to the bed.

Then he put her suitcase on the stand by the dresser. ''Why don't you rest while I make a few calls to see if the car I rented was delivered?''

She supposed Blake wanted to drive himself around L.A. That didn't surprise her. She didn't want to rest, though. She wanted him to kiss her. But hopefully that would come this evening.

A few hours later, Jenna decided everything about the evening was perfect. They ate at a fine restaurant where the maître d' showed Blake to a table where they could look down on the lights of the city. After Blake ordered lobster tail and filet mignon, they talked about Gary's dreams and what this weekend could mean to him. As conversation ebbed and flowed, their gazes meeting and holding often, Blake explained he'd already started a fund for their son or daughter's education. They ate the succulent lobster and superbly done steak and spoke of places they'd seen. Her experience was much more limited than Blake's, but she described a spot in northern California where her father had taken her and Gary one summer. A relaxed air settled over Blake as he painted word pictures of the scenery in the Greek Isles, the beauty of Norway, the old world marvels of Italy. Time spun away from them and it didn't seem to matter.

For dessert Blake ordered strawberry cheesecake, and she remembered again the teddy bear now sitting on the rocker in the nursery along with all the kind and wonderful things Blake had done since she'd met him. Didn't that mean he cared for her a little? Fingering her wedding band, she thought about their vows and what she'd promised.

With her cheesecake only half finished, she pushed it away. "I've had enough."

"We could take the rest back to the hotel, but—" He stopped. "How would you like to go for a walk on a private beach? It's about a forty-five-minute drive."

They'd gotten up early this morning and driven all day, but she wasn't about to say no to Blake now. A walk on the beach would be so romantic. "I'd like that."

In Blake's rental car, Jenna realized immediately they were headed for Malibu. He switched on the CD player and string medleys of slow ballads poured from the speakers. She hummed along with some of them as they drove, and she saw Blake smile. After they exited the freeway, she couldn't keep track of the turns and stopped trying.

Finally, he pulled up to a low-slung bungalow fashioned in stucco.

"Does this belong to a friend?" she asked softly.

"No. It belongs to me."

Her pulse raced as Blake climbed out, took off his jacket and tugged off his tie, throwing them in the back of the car. "I'm going to get a blanket from the trunk. It's a beautiful night, and we might want to sit and listen to the ocean."

Jenna's heart was beating so fast when Blake joined her again, it sounded louder than the waves breaking on the shore. Apparently Blake had prepared for tonight.

He took her arm as they stepped over sea grass and dunes, holding her securely so she wouldn't fall. When they reached the beach, his hand slid to hers and he laced their fingers. The gesture was so perfectly right.

As they walked, she asked, "Do you have homes anywhere else?"

"I have a condo in Vail and a property in Montana I'd like to build on someday. It's near Billings."

"You're full of surprises tonight."

"Don't you like surprises?" His voice was husky, his gray eyes intense under the light of the moon.

"I guess I've always been a very ordered person, but it's not too late to change," she said, remembering the conversation they'd had on the subject.

Stopping, he faced her and released her hand. "I want to surprise you with so many new things...new places."

"Why?" she asked softly, knowing it was a risk.

Blake let the blanket drop to the ground as he took her face between his hands. "Because you're the gentlest, most caring woman I know."

Those weren't the words she'd hoped for. As he bent his head and drew her lips up to his, she knew she had to make a decision that would affect the rest of her life. She loved Blake Winston. She could wait forever and he might never love her. But if she gave herself to him, sincerely tried to be the best mother and wife she knew how to be, in time he might come to love her.

That was the thought that seduced her as much as Blake's lips. Giving herself to him was like falling into a whirlpool of passion that filled her world. His kiss was hungrier than it had ever been and left her clinging to him.

Breaking away, he stared into her eyes and removed the pins from her upswept hair one by one.

"Do you know how long it took me to get it that

way?'' she asked shakily, holding on to sanity by the edge of her fingertips.

''I like your hair down around your face. I like running my fingers through it. I like burying my hands in it while I kiss you.'' And then that's what he did.

The waves slapped the shore in a rhythm as basic as his kiss. His tongue played against hers until she learned the game, then he groaned because he'd taught her too well.

Tearing himself away from her again, he held her shoulders. ''I want to make you mine—here…now.''

It was something she had never even contemplated, making love with a man on a beach at the edge of the world.

''There's no one around for miles,'' he reassured her. ''I'll spread the blanket on the softer sand.''

If she said yes to this, she was saying yes to Blake's world, to the sensuality he wanted to share with her, to the desire that had woven its threads around them from the moment they'd met. She loved him, and now she just had to wait until he loved her. The moon and the sky and the sea would be their witnesses as she pledged herself to him in a way she hadn't on their wedding day.

Touching his face—she'd never done that before— she traced her fingers lightly over his cheekbone, then smiled up at him. ''Spread the blanket on the sand.''

Still, he didn't move to do it. His voice was thick and husky as he asked, ''Are you sure? We can go up to the house. We can go back to the hotel.''

''In two separate rooms?''

''If that's what you want. Damn it, Jenna, I want you more than anything I've ever wanted in my life, except maybe this child. I won't jeopardize what we *do* have going for us.''

He wouldn't jeopardize having custody of his baby; he wouldn't jeopardize a marriage that was fragile. Did he think the wrong word or move could pull it apart? She hoped that wasn't the case. Those weren't the kind of promises she'd made.

She'd have to show him that. ''I want to be here…right now…with you. I want to make this marriage a true marriage.''

That was as plainly as she could put it without telling him she loved him. She sensed he wasn't ready to hear that yet. He didn't believe in love, and she had to convince him that it was as real as what they were going to do and prove it could last forever.

He leaned his forehead against hers and drew in a breath. Then he stepped back, pulled out his shirttails and quickly unfastened the buttons. She watched as he dropped the shirt to the sand and then spread the blanket before them. He was so comfortable with this, so experienced.

When he saw her expression, he stopped. ''What's wrong?''

She didn't want to spoil the mood. She didn't want to let her insecurities tumble out.

''I know what you're thinking,'' he said softly. ''But I've never done this before. I mean…here…like this…on a beach. With you, Jenna, everything is different. Everything is new.'' Coming to her then, he pulled her into his embrace and kissed her slowly and thoroughly like a man who wanted to make love to her more than anything else in the world. She believed Blake was an honest man, and to imagine that this was his first time like this—

When he leaned back, he began unfastening the buttons on her tunic, one tiny button at a time. "A man could go crazy doing this," he muttered.

She laughed and offered, "I can help."

"The only help I want tonight is for you to tell me what you like, what feels good, what we can do."

"We can do anything." She felt suddenly free, as if her world had broken up into colors and light, and love had rushed in.

Her tunic open now, he pushed it from her shoulders and it fell to the sand. Taking her hand, he eased her down onto the blanket with him. She watched him undress first as if he knew it would help her feel more comfortable. Then he helped her with the rest of her clothes until they both lay naked on the blanket, the ocean breaking fifty yards away, the black sky and full moon creating a canopy just for them.

As they lay face-to-face, Blake didn't give Jenna time to have second thoughts. He wanted to fill her world tonight. He wanted her to forget B.J. Winton. From her reaction, from her background, he guessed she'd never done anything like this before, and that was a good start. When he stroked her shoulder, he felt the quiver run through her. He knew he'd have to keep a tight rein on his self-control. In spite of his reputation, it had been a long time since he'd been with a woman…since he'd *wanted* to be with a woman. Physical pleasure had been enough impetus when he was younger, but for the past couple of years, it had seemed more trouble than it was worth. His time had been better spent working…or so he'd thought.

Until he'd met Jenna.

Now he wanted to give her pleasure as she'd never known. He wanted physical satisfaction and to satisfy some intangible yearning that had begun the first moment he'd looked into her eyes. Tonight would do that. Tonight would make everything easier.

"You're beautiful," he whispered, meaning it as he touched her breast and then her belly where his baby lay.

"I feel big," she murmured into his neck.

His palm slid over her satiny skin. "The only place you're big is here, and I'm glad of that."

She'd used perfume tonight. She was lilacs and summer, sweetness and freshness, along with innocence he'd never touched before. Although Jenna had been married, he sensed she didn't know what true pleasure was. He'd given her a taste of it on the boat. Now he wanted to give her so much more.

When he kissed her neck, a small sigh escaped her lips. As he journeyed further down, her hands caressed his arms and he didn't think anything could be more erotic.

His mouth neared her breast and he could feel her body tighten. Raising his head, he asked, "Do you like this?"

"Oh, yes."

Smiling, he brought his lips to her nipple, slid his tongue around it again and again until she was restless and hot. Then he rimmed the nipple and teased it until it was hard, until her fingers dug into his flesh, until he knew he was doing this right. Sliding his hand between her legs, he caressed and stroked her thigh, first one and then the other. She was opening to him, blossoming for him.

"Blake," she moaned, and he kissed her as he stroked her into a frenzy.

"I don't want to hurt you," he said as he knew the time was drawing nearer to complete their union.

"You won't. Oh, Blake, I need you."

He needed her, too. Pulling her leg over his hip, he slowly...ever so slowly...slid into her warmth, into the heat, and experienced satisfaction as he'd never known. He'd always used a condom before. He'd always taken precautions. Now he knew the pure pleasure of a woman's body and almost drowned in it.

"You feel so wonderful," she murmured, and he felt his control being swept away.

When he moved inside her, she gripped him tightly and his groan was deep, coming from his soul. He started moving faster then, hanging on to everything he'd known. But his iron grip loosened with every stroke until his hands opened and he was letting go, giving in, bestowing on Jenna the pleasure they both sought and needed. Desire built upon desire until passion was a concept he'd never understood until now. He wanted to reach the end of the journey, yet he wanted it to go on forever.

Jenna met every one of his thrusts with a welcoming of her body until they were rocking in a rhythm as primitive as the sand and water and sky. Their unleashed hunger for each other built and built and built until the cataclysmic explosion was imminent.

"Let yourself go," he urged Jenna as he touched the bud that threw her over the edge.

She called his name in a long, joyous cry that released any chains still binding him to earth. When he followed her into color and sensation and motion, her name was a mantra on his lips, and he finally felt that the child she was carrying would be truly his.

* * *

A short time later, they both floated back down to earth, and she lay with Blake's arm around her as they stared up at the moon.

"I don't want to go back," he said against her temple. "But with Gary there, we have to."

"I know." She was almost afraid to talk as if it would spoil what had happened between them. Yet nothing could spoil that. It had been perfect. Her fingers smoothed over the scar at his side, and she relived again the moment when she'd realized she loved him.

"Do you want to take a quick look at the house before we go back?"

"I'd like that."

Jenna knew Blake didn't share his emotions easily so she wasn't surprised when he was quiet as they walked back to the house, hand in hand. There was a definite change between them, a lessening of tension, a heightening of who they were together.

When she stepped inside his house, she was struck immediately by all the gleaming polished oak, the huge glass picture window facing the ocean. There was a long cushiony sofa and two rockers grouped in front of the fireplace. The off-white-and-stainless-steel kitchen gleamed.

"This is beautiful, Blake."

"It belonged to one of my first clients. He wanted something closer to the city and not so isolated. It was perfect for me."

She turned slowly, taking it all in. Then she asked, "Do you mind if I freshen up before we go back?"

"Feel free."

When she emerged from the bathroom fifteen minutes later, he was in the living room. He'd changed into jeans and a T-shirt and she'd never seen him look quite that casual or consummately sexy. He was still so quiet, though, and now that bothered her.

"I feel overdressed," she said lightly.

He looked as if he were about to say something, but then he just shrugged. "I still keep a few clothes here for when I'm in the area." He checked his watch. "We'd better get back."

That old guardedness was cropping up again and she wanted to say something to break through it. "I had a wonderful time tonight, Blake."

Still he didn't come close to her. "I pressured you into tonight, didn't I?"

So *that's* what was wrong. "You set the stage."

"I thrust you into a situation where it was practically impossible for you to say no."

Taking a few steps closer to him, she lifted her chin. "If I had wanted to say no, I would have said no. I could have asked you to take me back to the hotel after dinner instead of bringing me here."

Mowing his hand through his hair, he looked troubled. "I don't want you to regret tonight."

"I won't regret tonight. It was wonderful. *You* were wonderful."

After studying her carefully for a moment, he pulled her into his arms and gave her a stunningly demanding kiss. "I want you all over again."

"Then we'd better get back to the hotel," she said with a smile.

Blake glanced over at Jenna often as they drove back to L.A. She could feel his gaze on her and she wondered what he was thinking. As they took the elevator to their suite, the hotel was still vibrant with activity.

When they entered their living room, Blake asked, "Would you like something from room service?"

"After that meal?" she asked with a small laugh.

Approaching her, he folded his arms around her. "I thought we could ease back into undressing each other." Then his arms stiffened and he leaned away. "Unless you've changed your mind."

Was he so unsure of her? Or unsure of himself? "I haven't changed my mind. But I'd better try to get in touch with Gary first."

They both looked toward the phone and saw that the red light was blinking. "I'll bet that's him." Blake crossed to the desk. "I turned my cell phone off tonight, but there weren't any messages on it when I checked after we came back from the beach."

After he dialed for messages, he listened for what seemed to be a very long time. At first he smiled and then his expression became very serious.

When he hung up the phone, he explained, "Gary said he and his roommate had conferences with Peter about their work. He and Tom are writing a script together tonight and want to get together somehow before school starts to finish it. All of the seminar students are having breakfast with Peter at 7:00 a.m. so he thinks he'll be ready to leave by nine. I'll call him to let him know we got his message. If he and Tom are writing, they should still be up. It's just after midnight."

As Jenna crossed the room to stand by Blake at the phone, she asked, "Was that the only message?"

After a moment's pause, he answered her. "No. Senator Evanston called. I knew he was in L.A. this weekend and I'd left this number. He's planning an unexpected appearance and speech at a Chamber of Commerce meeting in Sacramento on Tuesday. He wants me to handle it."

"Isn't that short notice?"

"I've already put security teams together in an afternoon. The thing is—he wants me to personally be his bodyguard."

She was horrified after what had just happened to Blake less than three weeks ago. "You're not going to, are you?"

"Yes, I am."

Panic seemed to claim her. "Blake, you can't. You put yourself in danger for him once, isn't that enough?"

"He never thought the threat would become a reality. Since he feels I saved his life, he wants me beside him again. It's not so unusual. He's using me like a good-luck charm."

"You can delegate someone else. I don't want you to do this. What if the man who went after him wasn't working alone?"

Blake shook his head. "There's no indication he was involved in a conspiracy. Don't you think I've investigated this thoroughly? So have the authorities. The man who attacked him is a misguided fanatic whose political opinions are opposite of Evanston's. *This* appearance of Evanston's will just be a run-of-the-mill operation."

Jenna felt quick tears come to her eyes as she turned away from Blake so he wouldn't see them. She'd just found him. She didn't want to lose him. She'd never thought of his work as dangerous, but now—

Suddenly his hands were on her shoulders and he was nudging her around. "This is a special case, Jenna, but this is the work I do. Most of the time it's about computers and alarms and putting a good team together. In this instance I feel I have to give my client the additional emotional security he needs. It will be fine. I promise you.''

''You can't make a promise like that,'' she whispered.

Lifting her chin, he looked deep into her eyes. ''Trust me, Jenna. Trust me when I say that no one will get near me or Senator Evanston this time.''

She wanted to believe that, but she didn't know if she could. Reluctantly disentangling herself from his arms, yet still troubled, she lifted the receiver of the phone. ''I'm going to call Gary.''

''I'll be in my bedroom,'' Blake told her, leaving the choice of what she wanted to do next tonight up to her.

Jenna tried to give her brother her full attention, enjoying his excitement and enthusiasm, seeing how much this weekend had meant to him. They decided to meet in the lobby the next morning at nine-thirty. After she wished him a good-night, she knew he'd probably be up all night with his roommate. That's what this weekend had been about. Her father wanted him to get a well-rounded education, and she thought that was best, too. If he could incorporate filmmaking into the rest, maybe their dad wouldn't have such a hard time with it.

After her conversation with Gary, she went to her room and took a quick shower. Thinking about Blake and Senator Evanston again, she decided she couldn't argue with Blake about his work or place demands on him simply because she was worried. She did have to trust him. Wasn't trust the basis of marriage as much as love?

Leaving her nightgown folded in the drawer, she put on her robe and went to Blake's room. His door was open and she could hear him talking on the phone.

"I'll handle all of it personally, but Al Bailey will be one-hundred-percent involved. No one else will know every aspect of the operation...they'll just know their part in it. Let's meet Monday morning, and Al and I will both explain it to you." There was a pause, then he said, "Good night, Senator."

When Blake put the cell phone on the nightstand, he saw her standing in the doorway. After his gaze came alight with silver fire, she could have sworn someone switched on electricity that snapped between them.

"Come here," he said with a crook of his finger. His voice was husky, and it was a request more than a demand.

Crossing to him, she stopped a few inches from him. "I know the work you do is important, but after what happened to you, I can't help but be afraid."

"I'm good at what I do, Jenna. It's a combination of instinct, know-how and pure sweat." He reached up and slowly trailed his fingers up and down her arms. "But right now, I'd rather sweat because of something other than work."

As his thumb trailed down the lapels of her robe, she shivered.

"Cold?" he asked, though his eyes said he knew better.

She shook her head. "I have all kinds of reactions when you touch me."

As he scooped her up into his arms, she gasped and asked, "What are you doing?"

"Carrying you to bed. Isn't that where you want to go?"

"Yes, but—"

"We're going to forget everything except how good we can make each other feel."

After he gently laid her on the bed, he quickly shucked off his clothes and then lay beside her. As he pushed her robe from her shoulders, she remembered everything he had done to her a few hours before and she gave herself into his care once again.

A long time later, both replete from their loving, sleepy from being physically spent, she lay curled beside Blake, her head on his shoulder. "You're such a wonderful lover," she murmured, remembering his tenderness, his gentleness and his passion.

He brought his hand to her tummy and let it settle there. "Tonight I feel as if I'm truly this child's father."

Jenna's repletion and sleepiness faded with his words. Apparently being a father was more important than being her husband. Had she pleased him, or had tonight been all about claiming her so he could claim his child?

Blake's child.

She no longer thought of this baby as B.J.'s. She hadn't thought of B.J. all evening…but she was thinking about him now. How much time had to pass before she would feel as if she truly belonged to Blake? How much time had to pass before B.J. would simply be a memory? He was still part of her and she didn't know if that would ever change.

A little voice in her head whispered, *If Blake truly loved you, your marriage to B.J. would fade into the past.*

With her cheek pressed to Blake's strong shoulder, she closed her eyes knowing her dreams tonight would be of Blake and the future they could share.

Chapter Thirteen

When Jenna awakened Monday morning, she reached across the bed...and found Blake gone. Then she remembered. He had an early meeting in Sacramento. She thought about the weekend all over again, the long drive home, and how Gary had been so excited about everything that had happened. Though the drive in the limousine had been comfortable, she'd been so tired last night. Blake had seen that and invited her into his bed for a massage. It had been wonderful. *He* had been wonderful. She'd almost fallen asleep under his hands. Afterward, he'd simply gathered her into his arms and they'd slept together. He seemed to like holding her.

Yet she couldn't forget his words—*Tonight I feel as if I'm truly this child's father.*

She had to prove to Blake that she wanted to move forward with him, that she wanted their life together. Her feelings for B.J. didn't have to be a stumbling block if she could prove to Blake she was committed to him and their marriage.

Sitting up on the edge of the bed, Jenna still felt so tired. She could see her ankles were a bit swollen, but that wasn't unusual at this stage of pregnancy. She had a month until her due date…a month until she held her baby in her arms. She had an appointment with her doctor the day after tomorrow.

Jenna had no intention of letting fatigue dictate her day. She wanted to call Blake and wish him good morning, but his meeting with Senator Evanston was important. She was worried about it, worried about Blake acting as a personal bodyguard, worried that another threat had come up that Blake wasn't telling her about. Yet she couldn't let her anxiety turn her into an oversolicitous wife. During B.J.'s illness, her faith had kept her strong. Now she'd rely on that faith to guide her through her new marriage.

As Jenna dressed, she arranged her day. The first thing she was going to do was drop off the settlement papers at Rafe's office. She would accept the clinic's offer, then pay off the rest of B.J.'s medical bills, help Gary with college tuition and maybe donate the rest. That's what Blake had done with his. If they had a true marriage, she didn't need the money. She was still determined to teach some way, somehow. But after the baby was born, she and her husband could discuss the best way she could do that.

Fatigue continued to plague Jenna as she drove to Rafe's office and handed the papers to his secretary. He was in court and wouldn't be back until afternoon. Jenna assured the woman she didn't need to see him. He could call her if there was anything to discuss.

Next on Jenna's agenda was a visit to her father.

Last evening when she and Blake had taken Gary home, there'd been a note on the refrigerator. Her father and Shirley had gone to an outdoor concert. Gary had given her a conspiratorial wink, and Jenna had hoped her father was going to be able to find love in his life after such a long time. She wanted to find out more about his "date" as well as get his opinion on Gary's reaction to the weekend.

The kitchen was empty when Jenna pushed open the back door, but there was an apple pie cooling on the counter and the scent of cinnamon and nutmeg filled the house. "Hello, anybody home?" Jenna called, but there was no answer.

The drone of a voice came from somewhere deeper in the house. Going down the hall, she found both her father's office and his study were dark, but she could hear the voice more clearly now. It sounded like Gary's.

When she stepped into the living room, she saw her father sitting on the sofa, intently watching a video on the TV. Gary's voice moderated the film, and she suspected it was his project from the weekend.

Her father looked up at her, and she couldn't tell from his expression what he was thinking. Instead of interrupting, she sat on the sofa beside him and watched with him. Although Gary had told her about the short documentary, she hadn't actually seen it.

"This is good," her father said with amazement in his voice as his eyes never left the TV screen. "Have you seen this?"

"No. Gary told us about it, but I haven't viewed it."

The videotape was silent now as Gary let the camera do the talking for him. He'd shot the footage at a beach. A little boy about three who only had one arm was trying to build a sand castle. There was frustration on the child's face as one of his turrets toppled over. But then as he carefully packed sand with his hand, thumped it into exactly the right spot and lifted off the bucket, there was such pride on his face. Jenna felt her throat tighten.

She and her father watched the footage through to the end and then he switched off the TV and the VCR. "Gary left it on the kitchen table this morning before he went to work," her father told her.

"That was an invitation for you to watch it."

"I guessed that. When I got home last night…" Her dad shook his head. "I've never seen him so exuberant, so enthused about anything. This weekend Winston offered him could have been a huge mistake."

"Didn't you just say the work he did was good?"

"*Good* won't get him what he wants. A career in film, Jenna. That's only going to lead to disappointment."

Through the years she and Gary had championed each other, and now was the time to do it once more. "And what if he *is* a success? What if he's persistent and dedicated enough to outshine everyone else, to get people to take notice? *You* noticed. From what he told us, Peter Selanki noticed. That man is well respected in his field."

Her dad ran his hand through his thinning gray-brown hair. "Success isn't all it's cracked up to be. There are temptations that go with it, and a man is better off without them."

All these years, Jenna had thought her father didn't want Gary to pursue a career in moviemaking because of the lifestyle it would lead to. But now it sounded as if there were more to it, as if he knew personally what those temptations were.

"You sound as if you know all about it."

"I *do* know about it. My life isn't as insular as you think."

"I know there's a lot you've never told me."

Her father grunted. "A man doesn't like to talk about his failures and his mistakes, especially to his children."

"You haven't told us very much at all. I'm an adult now. I think I could understand anything you have to say. I think I could have understood even when I was younger."

"Understood what?"

"How much you missed Mom." B.J.'s death had brought it all back, although she hadn't realized it at the time. One loss had seemed to compound the other.

Her father's voice was thick as he said, "I didn't want it to be worse for you and Gary. Back then, I thought not talking about your mom's death kept us all from being sad. Since then in workshops I've taken, I've learned I was wrong. One of the many mistakes I mentioned."

"You can talk about her now," Jenna offered softly.

After a long moment, he asked, "Do you remember anything about her?"

Jenna closed her eyes to pull her memories into focus. "I remember she had eyes as blue as the sky. I remember she had a sweet, sweet voice…and at Christmas…I can almost hear her singing 'Silent Night'."

"That was her favorite carol. Pink was her favorite color. And her smile…" He shook his head. "Her smile lit up my world. When she died, the lights went out for me for a long time. I couldn't show you and

Gary how much I missed her, or I might not have been able to go on. You were a trouper helping with Gary the way you did.''

Her father had thanked her for helping to raise Gary on her wedding day to B.J. That was one of those moments she'd cherish for a lifetime.

"But she *is* gone, Dad. Just like B.J.'s gone."

In an unprecedented gesture, her father took her hand in his. "I know how hard these past few years have been for you since B.J. was diagnosed. This marriage you've entered into so hastily—"

"Dad, I love Blake."

Her father looked shocked. "I thought you did this out of duty! I thought you did it for the child. How could you possibly love him so soon?"

Her father might be stoic much of the time, but she knew he was a man of deep convictions and deep emotions. Otherwise, he still wouldn't be missing her mother. "How long did it take you to fall in love with Mom?"

Startled by the question, he thought about it. "No time at all. After a service, she complimented me on my sermon. I looked into those blue eyes…. It took me a while to work up the courage to ask her out, but before the movie was over, I knew I wanted her to be my wife."

"It wasn't like that with me and B.J.," Jenna admitted. "There wasn't a lot of lightning or fireworks. I realize now…B.J. and I never had the passion between us that Blake and I have. Yet B.J. and I knew we could trust each other. We knew we'd always be there for each other. And even though I love Blake now, I'm having trouble letting go. Maybe I still feel

I'm betraying B.J. somehow. I don't know. Do you have any advice?''

Her father grimaced. "I'm supposed to have all the answers, aren't I? As a father…as a minister. But I don't. Maybe now that you're an adult, I can admit that to you. I certainly never would have picked Blake Winston for a husband for you.''

"But he *is* my husband. He's a fine man, Dad. You'd find that out if you'd get to know him.''

The conversation was interrupted by footsteps in the hall. Seconds later, Shirley peeked into the living room. "I'm sorry if I interrupted.''

Charles stood. "It's okay, Shirley. Do you need help bringing the groceries in?''

"That would be nice.''

It was easy to see something was different between Shirley and her father. It was in their expressions when they looked at each other. "How was the concert last night?'' Jenna asked.

"It was wonderful,'' Shirley said at the same time as her father admitted, "Very nice.''

"What were the selections? Classical, popular?''

Both Shirley and her dad exchanged a look. "Some of both, I think,'' Shirley answered.

"We were talking some of the time,'' her father said by way of explanation for their inattention to the concert.

Jenna couldn't hide a smile.

"Would you like to stay for lunch?'' Shirley motioned to the kitchen. "I bought plenty at the deli.''

Rising to her feet, Jenna declined. "No, I have more errands to run. I'd like to stop at the school and see if the teachers are getting their classrooms ready. I also want to stop at the maternity shop.'' She wanted to buy a new nightgown, something Blake would like. It was an extravagance since she only had a month to wear it, but she felt it would be worth it.

"It's already a hundred degrees out there," Shirley warned. "Be careful. Let your car cool off before you get inside."

Jenna hugged her dad. To her surprise, he put his arms around her and hugged her back.

Thinking about her brother, she insisted, "We'll talk about Gary again later. Just remember, he's doing what he loves to do, just like you're doing the work you love to do. That's important."

Then she smiled at Shirley and went on with moving her life forward.

Jenna's visit with a few of her friends at school made her miss the work *she* loved. Maybe once the baby was born, she could tutor students. After an hour or so, she said her goodbyes and went out to her car, forgetting about Shirley's warning. As soon as she got inside, she was sorry she had. Even though she'd left the window open, it really did feel like an oven and she was suddenly dizzy. As she started the car, the air-conditioning began to blow and she aimed it into her face. In a few minutes, cooler air pumped through. Leaning her head back against the seat, she took a few deep breaths. When she straightened at the wheel again, the wooziness passed. Should she call her father or Marilyn?

She hated to do that when she was feeling fine now. If she felt the least bit dizzy again while she was driving, she'd pull over and use her cell phone. The maternity shop would have to wait.

By the time she got home, she was simply hot and her feet felt swollen. She removed her sandals as soon as she stepped into the house. Carrying them to the kitchen, she found a note from Marilyn.

Went to the hairdresser and shopping. Be back to serve dinner at seven.

Peering inside the refrigerator, Jenna decided she wasn't hungry, just thirsty. Pouring herself a glass of iced herbal tea, she knew how she was going to spend the afternoon. She had one last box in her closet to sort through from her move here. Once she did that, she'd feel as if her life was really in order. Maybe tonight, Blake could help her transfer the last of her things from her room to his. She was feeling more like his wife every day. If only he could let down his barriers...

Once upstairs, Jenna slid the box out of her closet. It was too heavy to lift. She flipped open the flaps and gathered the top third of the contents, taking them to the chair by the bed. After she set the two photograph albums with assorted programs and cards on the bed, she went through them, one by one. An hour later, she hadn't gone much farther. These were mementos from the first years of her marriage—pictures, cards, ticket stubs. She relived her first date with B.J. and every first thereafter.

As her tears slowed, she blew her nose and began thinking about her "firsts" with Blake—their first meeting, their first kiss, the first time they made love.

Made love.

She wanted and needed Blake's love. Would he ever be able to give it?

Blake came home at four o'clock and smiled to himself as he went to the kitchen to get something cold to drink. This was the earliest he'd been home from work in years. He'd been out of the house before six this morning, and he'd missed talking to Jenna. He'd missed kissing Jenna. She was such an integral part of his life now.

He saw the note from Marilyn as he grabbed a can of soda, then noticed Jenna's purse on the foyer table. She was probably upstairs—resting, he hoped. She'd been tired after their busy weekend. He smiled again. *Busy* wasn't quite the word for it.

When the phone rang, he picked it up before it was finished the first ring. "Winston here."

"Winston? It's Rafe Pierson. Is Jenna there?"

The two men hadn't spoken since Blake had married Jenna. He didn't know what the Piersons thought of Jenna's marriage, though it hadn't seemed to change Shannon's friendship with his wife.

He found himself wanting to get to know the couple better, for Jenna's sake as well as his. "I think she's napping. I don't want to disturb her if she is."

Rafe seemed to hesitate for a few seconds. "No, don't disturb her. It's not that important. My secretary gave me the papers she signed and dropped off for the settlement. I just wanted her to know I have them and I'll deliver them to the clinic personally tomorrow. I should have a check for her by the end of the day."

Blake's buoyant mood sank a few notches. Jenna hadn't told him she'd signed the papers. She hadn't told him she was going ahead with the settlement. What was she going to do with the money? It didn't matter to him...except—

What if she planned to squirrel it away as an insurance policy in case their marriage didn't work out? A hundred thousand dollars could take her and their baby far away. *You shouldn't even be thinking it,* a wise voice inside him challenged. Yet an old tape played with unrestrained clarity. Danielle had chosen money and education and freedom over him. Might not Jenna?

Not betraying any of his feelings to Rafe, he said evenly, "I'll make sure she gets the message."

There was an awkward silence until Rafe filled it. "Do you like horseback riding?"

The question seemed to come out of left field. "I used to ride in L.A. once in a while. Why?"

"I thought maybe sometime you might like to try out one of our horses here, go on a real trail ride. You and me. I thought it might be a good idea to mend fences, and maybe get to know each other better."

To his surprise, Blake liked that idea. "I'll give you a call this weekend and we can set something up."

"Sounds good," Rafe said.

When Blake hung up, he saw how his life was changing…because of Jenna.

After he drank the soda, he climbed the stairs and went to his bedroom, hoping to find Jenna there. But his suite was empty. The door to her room was ajar, though. What he found at first startled him…then frustrated him…then angered him. She'd obviously been crying. A box of tissues sat on the floor by her chair. The bed was littered with memorabilia and at a glance, he could tell what all of it was from—her marriage to B.J. Winton. She was surrounded by it…pictures and ribbons and pressed flowers.

He thought they'd come further than this. He thought the weekend had been important…that he'd claimed her as his. But now, seeing the expression on her tear-stained face—

"Blake! You're home early."

"I thought you'd be taking a nap," he said in a low voice, controlling the squall of emotions inside of him.

"I'm...I'm sorting—"

"You're not sorting, Jenna, you're wallowing in a marriage that's over...done...gone." He couldn't believe the fury he was struggling to rein in.

"Don't you think I know it's over, Blake? I'm married to *you* now."

"No, I don't think you are. You're still married to *him*. Your wedding band, the marriage ceremony, the weekend we spent in L.A. obviously didn't change that."

Her brown eyes were moist with emotion that he thought was all for B.J. "I want our marriage, Blake, as much as I want our child. But I can't erase the memories. I can't pretend I have amnesia and B.J. never existed."

"How I wish you *did* have amnesia." Detaching himself from Jenna and everything they'd shared, he remembered the message from her lawyer. "Pierson called. By tomorrow afternoon, you'll have a check for one hundred thousand dollars. Or did he do some private negotiating I don't know about and the clinic upped the ante?"

"He didn't do any negotiating."

She looked upset now and he was sorry about that, but they had to deal with reality. He *had* to deal with it the same way he had after Danielle betrayed him, the same way he had after his mother and then his father died.

Motioning to the bits of Jenna's life spread out on the bed, he couldn't keep his accusation inside. "I wonder if you were going to tell me at all. A hundred thousand dollars could give you a good start somewhere. Maybe you think you and your baby can disappear. Let me tell you, Jenna, wherever you take my child, I'll find you.''

''I had no intention of leaving!''

He didn't know whether to believe her or not. She'd gone back in time without him, and he was just as afraid she'd go forward without him. ''I once told you I didn't trust anyone. I still don't. Whether you're telling the truth or not remains to be seen. But I do know one thing.'' He picked up an open photograph album and then slammed it back down on the bed. ''If you continue with this kind of thing, if you continue feeding your memories of B.J. Winton, we'll never have a marriage.''

Rising to her feet now, she took a bolstering breath. ''Maybe I could pack all this away and forget about it if I knew—'' She stopped abruptly. ''Tell me something, Blake, why did you marry me?''

There was no easy answer to that one, and he responded out of the pain coming into this room and seeing her figuratively wrapped in B.J. Winton's arms had brought him. Eyeing her belly, he said in a voice devoid of emotion, ''That's obvious.''

He saw the pain his defensive words inflicted and yet he was powerless to go to her. He'd armored himself well against any attachment, but somehow Jenna had gotten through that armor. He had to patch it up again. ''I'm going back to the office. I'll stay in Sacramento tonight. I have to be there early again for the final run-through for security on Evanston's speech. If you need anything, Marilyn will be back later, and you can always call me.''

As he had recognized from the beginning, Jenna was no fragile flower. Her shoulders squared and her dark eyes spoke of her independence. "I won't need you, Blake. I'll be fine."

They were at a stalemate and they both knew it. There wasn't anything more to say. "I'll be home late tomorrow night."

Maybe he would have put his life back in order by then. Maybe he could figure out how to parent a child with Jenna without wanting her.

He quickly left her room and the house to escape the pain of losing something he thought he'd found.

After Blake left, Jenna didn't know what to do. She sank into the bedroom chair, feeling stunned by everything that had happened. She'd wept earlier in the afternoon because the pictures, the memories of B.J., had been bittersweet. She'd wept because she wasn't sure Blake could ever love her the way she loved him. He'd walked in, taken in all of it and assumed she'd been wrapped up in the past.

Her feelings were complicated. Letting go was hard. Yet she recognized the underlying truth—she loved Blake Winston with a depth in which she'd never loved before.

His words haunted her. *A hundred thousand dollars could give you a good start somewhere. Maybe you think you and your baby can disappear.*

Why hadn't she told Blake she was going to sign the settlement papers? Maybe because she wanted to surprise him, just as she'd surprised him by ordering the baby furniture. She finally wanted to put the clinic's mistake behind them and prove to him she had.

But he'd thought she was trying to do something behind his back. He'd thought she was keeping a back door open so she could bail out. She didn't want to bail out! She loved him, and she longed to tell him so. Yet that had been the risk—declaring her love before she knew what he felt. All this time, she'd known he was protecting himself. She hadn't realized she was doing the same.

Was it too late?

Her head ached as she remembered the expression on his face. Her stomach hurt as she remembered his words and relived their argument. Blake still carried a burden of guilt about his father's death. But this afternoon *she'd* realized she carried guilt over B.J. Is that why she couldn't let go?

What if she could have convinced B.J. to have more chemo? What if he hadn't been concerned about her financial future? He might never have gotten well, but he'd sacrificed months of living because of expensive treatments, because he hadn't wanted her to see him suffer, because he'd been exhausted from fighting a disease that would take him, anyway.

There was no going back. She knew that. If she explained all this to Blake, maybe he would understand. It had just become harder and harder to talk to him about B.J., and now she knew why. Blake needed her whole heart and soul. He needed to be the only man in her life before he could trust her. How could she convince him the promises she'd made would last a lifetime?

By the time she'd packed everything on her bed in the carton again and pushed it into the back corner of the closet, her head was throbbing, her feet were still swollen, and she realized she hadn't put them up this afternoon because she'd become too engrossed in the past.

She had to take care of herself and the baby. She

had to calm some of the turmoil inside her before she became sick with it. Somehow she knew Blake wouldn't want to hear from her tonight or even tomorrow when his focus would be on Senator Evanston. She just hoped it wasn't too late to show Blake how much she loved him. Tomorrow night when he came home, she'd be waiting, all of her defenses down, ready to take a risk, willing to explain anything he needed for her to explain, eager to tell him how much she loved him.

Jenna buzzed Marilyn and told her Blake wouldn't be home until the following evening. Later, she tried to eat the meal Marilyn had prepared but couldn't. She was tied up in knots and her head still throbbed. After spending time in the baby's room, wondering if Marilyn would help her decorate the walls tomorrow, she went to bed.

It was a restless night and she missed Blake terribly—his scent and hard body next to hers, missed the huskiness in his voice whenever he spoke about their child. She almost called him in the middle of the night but realized how foolish that would be. He needed all his wits about him tomorrow. She was still worried about his stint as the senator's bodyguard tomorrow evening. Yet she knew Blake was good at what he did and his work was part of who he was. Trying to go back to sleep, she eventually dozed off.

When Jenna awakened in the morning, she knew something was terribly wrong. The persistent headache hadn't lessened. Not only were her feet swollen now, but her hands and her face, as well. She could tell by touching her hands to her cheeks.

When she tried to get up to go to the mirror, she felt

dizzy and she hit the intercom button instead. "Marilyn."

"Yes, Mrs. Winston."

"I think I need your help. I feel as if I'm going to...pass out...."

Now Jenna wished she had called Blake in the middle of the night. She wished she had told him...

A smothering gray fog surrounded her, though she fought it. It was a thick, heavy blanket, and as she slid to the floor, it enveloped her.

Chapter Fourteen

Rushing into Fawn Grove General Hospital, more afraid and panicked than he'd ever been, Blake found Reverend Seabring in the emergency room. Marilyn had phoned Blake; he'd phoned Jenna's father because he knew the reverend could get to Jenna before he could.

"Where is she?" he demanded.

"They rushed her upstairs to the operating room," Charles Seabring said solemnly. "I had to give permission for a C-section. The ER doctor said something about eclampsia."

Fear pounded Blake hard as he tried to remember everything he'd learned about the condition during the parenting classes. No one knew what caused it. Pre-eclampsia could develop into eclampsia. His mind was muddled as he remembered bits of facts—first-time pregnancies, hypertension, seizures. All of it was serious and could lead to death. Did Charles know that? When his gaze met Jenna's father's, he could see that he did.

"We'd better get upstairs." The reverend's voice was even, but Blake could sense the terror underneath.

The elevator seemed to take forever to rise three floors, and all the while Blake was blaming himself for this, too.

Apparently Charles had gotten directions from one of the nurses, and he led Blake to a waiting room. Jenna's father sank down onto one of the vinyl chairs, but Blake had to keep moving. He paced from one end of the room to the other, feeling like a caged lion, afraid that he was losing everything that mattered to him.

Charles didn't speak.

When Blake could no longer stand the cacophony of his own thoughts, he admitted, "This is my fault. This is all my fault."

"This is probably no one's fault."

It was possibly the hardest thing Blake had ever done, but he sat down next to Jenna's father and looked him straight in the eye. "You don't understand. We did all that driving last weekend. We…" He didn't know how to say this to a woman's father, but he just said it. "We consummated our marriage. To top it all off, we argued yesterday and I spent the night in my office in Sacramento. If I had been there last night—"

The look in Charles's eyes wasn't the condemning one Blake expected. "The night Jenna's mother died, Mary and I had the worst argument of our marriage. She saw what was happening to me in my church." He paused, then went on. "The congregation was a large one, and I was courting those members who donated the most money. My excuse was the funds would enable me to provide more services to the poor and needy, but Mary saw through that. She saw that my ego was getting bigger and bigger, seeing my name in the paper with important members of the community and sitting on instrumental boards had become more important to me than my work."

When he became silent, Blake didn't know what to say.

Jenna's dad continued. "She wanted me to leave Pasadena, take a post at a smaller church and do the work that had taken up all my time in the first years of our marriage. All I could see was that she wanted me to go backward, not forward. I said things I shouldn't have said. In the middle of the night, an aneurysm we never knew she had burst and she died before I could even tell her I loved her. For years I believed our argument caused her death."

"What did the doctor say?" Blake asked in a low voice.

"The doctors explained the aneurysm was a bomb waiting to explode. But I thought I knew better. Sometimes, Blake, we think we're much too powerful. Sometimes there's a plan we know nothing about. Mary's death brought me back to the work that gives my life meaning, and I've finally come to terms with all of it. As far as Jenna's concerned, the eclampsia might have happened whether you traveled or not, whether you argued or not. Then again, if you look at everything she's been through over the past few years—" He rubbed his brow. "I should have been kinder, I should have done more, I should have accepted you when she chose you."

"Did she choose me, or did she choose the best life for her child?" Blake asked.

Charles sat up straighter and looked uncomfortable, as if debating about what he was going to say. Then with the aplomb most ministers had in learning to deal with delicate subjects, he said, "She told me she loves you. And if as you said you and Jenna consummated your marriage this weekend, there's no doubt about it. If my Jenna did that, then she definitely loves you. Does she know *you* love *her?*"

Love Jenna?

Had he been dancing around the truth for the past two months, calling all that he was feeling everything *but* love? Yes, he had. And yes, he knew he loved her. If he had realized it sooner, this might not have happened.

All too well, Blake remembered what he'd told her last night when she asked him why he'd married her. "No, she doesn't know I love her. She thinks I married her for the baby. I thought I married her…" He didn't go into that, but Charles seemed to get the gist.

"If we let our defenses down a bit, maybe we could figure out what's going on inside of us. Women seem much more capable of doing that than men."

Defenses had been part of Blake's life for as far back as he could remember. Keeping them implacably in place was far safer than giving anyone power to get through them. In spite of himself, he'd given Jenna that power. He realized now the need and want he'd felt for her, the longing to keep her in his life was all part of being in love with her. He loved her so much that if anything happened to her now…

"Pray for her," he pleaded with Jenna's father.

"Ah, Blake." Charles's voice was kind. "Even if

you haven't done it in a while, you can pray as well as I can. If both of us storm heaven, maybe we'll have a better chance of getting through.''

Hoping Charles's words were true, Blake closed his eyes and prayed as he'd never prayed before.

Monitors beeped, ten voices seemed to be talking at once as Jenna tried to get her bearings and the gray fog dissipated. The problem was, none of it made any sense.

''We're losing her'' came a shout from below, and Jenna realized she was above all the activity and the noise and the lights. Whatever was happening—

''Jenna?'' a male voice called.

''Blake?'' She needed Blake. She longed for Blake. She yearned to be with him.

Then someone was standing beside her taking her hand. ''No. Not Blake. It's B.J.''

Though she'd heard his words first, now he came into focus. ''What are you doing here?''

''That's not the question,'' he said with that familiar grin. ''The question is what are *you* doing here?''

''I don't know. I—''

''You don't belong here, Jenna. It's not your time yet.''

''It wasn't your time, either! I should have convinced you to fight harder.''

''You're wrong about that. It *was* my time, and I knew it. No amount of treatments, no amount of love from you could have given me more than I had. But now you're ready for Blake.'' He held up their clasped hands. ''Let go of me, Jenna. Let go and hold on to Blake. He needs you and his daughter more than I ever could.''

She stared at her hand holding on to B.J.'s. The love for Blake that had been blossoming all these weeks became a full-blooming flower—rich, mature, over-powering. One by one, Jenna released each finger and moved away from B.J.

"Goodbye," she whispered, and felt no sorrow, only peace. Anticipation of fully embracing her love for Blake caused tingling in every atom of who she was. She felt as if she were floating, and then she heard the beep of monitors again and a low voice, very close to her.

"Come back to me, Jenna. Please." It was Blake's voice.

As she tried to move, she realized he was holding her hand. Her eyes fluttered open and she squeezed his fingers, letting him know she was back.

Finally, with much effort, she managed a whisper. "Blake?"

His face was filled with relief and then concern as he rose to call the doctor.

"No, wait." She didn't want him going anywhere. She didn't want him leaving her. She didn't want him letting go.

"I love you," she said in a much stronger voice. "I should have told you that yesterday, but I was afraid you wouldn't believe me. I had plans for the check and I was going to tell you about them. I wanted to put the clinic behind me…behind us. I wanted the rest of our lives to be about you and me, not about the clinic's mistake."

Sitting beside her again, Blake brought her hand to his lips and kissed it. "I've been protecting myself, Jenna. I've learned how to do it too well. I didn't think I even knew how to love anymore. But I guess we never lose the ability...if we meet the right person. If we open ourselves to the possibility.''

Tenderly he caressed her palm and held it so reverently, his gesture brought tears to her eyes. ''It wasn't until I thought I'd lost you that I realized how much I love you. When Marilyn called me this morning, I was afraid I *deserved* to lose you. I never should have left you last night. I love you, Jenna. Can you forgive all the mistakes I've made? Can you forgive what I said yesterday?''

When she removed her hand from his, she lovingly touched the stubble of his beard and smiled. ''I already have.''

He kissed her then, gently, lightly but fervently.

When he leaned away, she asked, ''How's our daughter?''

His jaw dropped. ''How did you know? They said they almost lost you. They said you were unconscious.''

''B.J. told me. I saw him, Blake, and I said goodbye. I love you so differently than I ever loved him—so much more richly, so much more maturely.'' She felt her cheeks pinken. ''So much more passionately.''

Blake looked as if she'd just handed him the world. ''I was a fool to be jealous of him,'' he said gruffly. ''I'm sorry, Jenna. You have every right to miss him...to grieve. I'll love you while you grieve...after you grieve...forever.''

In Blake's eyes she could see a vision of what they could have together...the sincerity and honesty of the promise he'd just made. ''I'm finished grieving. I'll remember B.J. always, but I'm finished missing him, too. You're my life now, Blake. You and our daughter are my future. Is she all right?'' Although she asked the question, there was a knowing in her soul that their baby would thrive as they would.

"Even though she's premature, she was still five pounds. It must have been those vitamins," Blake said with a smile. "The doctors are watching her carefully. They might keep her here a little longer than you. But she's beautiful, Jenna. She has lots of dark brown hair and huge eyes. She's going to look just like you."

"When can I come home?" she asked, wanting to be alone with Blake, wanting to be in their house, wanting to start their new life.

"You gave us a real scare and you had surgery."

"I don't want to be apart from you," she protested.

Then he gave her one of those Blake-smiles that turned her insides to mush. "I'll stay here with you tonight."

"Can you do that?"

"I'm on the hospital board. Besides that, I'm your husband. I won't let them kick me out."

And she knew he wouldn't. No one would make Blake Winston do anything he didn't want to do. "I love you," she told him again with so much feeling, tears once more filled her eyes.

Sliding into bed beside her, Blake took her into his arms and held her so tightly she knew he'd never let her go.

Epilogue

On Christmas Day, Blake hung Al and Sue Bailey's coats in the foyer closet while they joined Jenna in the living room with Rafe and Shannon and their girls, as well as Shannon's aunt Cora. When Blake had left his wife's side to answer the door, four-month-old Elizabeth Mary had been asleep in the cradle by the fireplace. Never before had he expected much of Christmas Day...never treated it differently from any weekend. But this year, everything was different. He'd never imagined he could be this happy. He'd never imagined he could feel so much love and give it freely to both Jenna and their daughter. Remembering the morning he'd sat in the hospital not knowing if Jenna and the baby would live or not, he'd vowed never to take them for granted again.

The doorbell pealed once more, and knowing that Marilyn was busy in the kitchen, Blake answered it himself. Jenna's father and brother stood there with smiles on their faces and presents in their arms. Jenna's dad and Shirley were officially keeping company now, but Shirley had gone to Washington to spend the holidays with her sisters.

"Good sermon last night, Reverend," Blake said to Charles as they set down the presents and he took their coats. He and Jenna hadn't lingered after midnight services last night because they'd wanted to get home to Elizabeth. After Jenna had given her father and brother a hug and Blake had wished them a merry Christmas, they'd come home to find Marilyn snoozing in the rocking chair in Elizabeth's room. She'd decided to be the little girl's guardian angel and was now more of a nanny than a housekeeper.

As Gary deposited his presents on a foyer chair, he told Blake, "My Christmas present is in the car. I can't wait to show it to you."

"What is it?" Blake asked.

"You'll see soon enough," the teenager assured him with a grin.

After Gary ran back outside, Charles didn't follow the sound of voices into the living room. Rather, he lingered until Blake had hung up the coats. "There was something I wanted to say to you last night, but I didn't get the chance."

Blake slid his hands into his trouser pockets. He and Charles had been on friendly footing since the baby had been born, but he never knew quite what to expect from the minister.

"First of all, I want you to call me Charles. Mr. Seabring or Reverend don't work anymore. We're family."

"All right," Blake said cautiously, pleased but sensing there was more to come.

"I was wrong about you and I wanted to say it to your face. I've told it to Jenna many times, but last night I realized that wasn't good enough. You've made her happier than I've ever seen her. And the way you spoil my granddaughter…" Charles shook his head and grinned. "No other little girl could be so lucky."

"Thank you…Charles," Blake said before he called the man Reverend as he had the past few months. That day in the hospital he'd almost felt as if he had a father again. Charles Seabring was as complicated as the next man, but Blake was enjoying getting to know him.

Interrupting any awkwardness that might have come with the apology, Gary bounded back into the foyer, a camcorder in his hand. "Just look at this, will you? It's got *everything*."

Taking the camcorder, Blake examined it properly while Gary beamed and Charles looked a bit sheepish. "It's a creative outlet for him. It's better if he's filming rather than spending time in a pool hall."

Blake almost laughed out loud—as if Gary would ever spend time in a pool hall.

A few minutes later, after Blake introduced Gary and Charles to everyone else in the living room, he crossed to Jenna, took her by the hand, and said, "Excuse us, everyone. I need my wife out in the hall for a minute."

Jenna's eyes were questioning. But after she glanced at their daughter and saw she was sleeping peacefully, she followed Blake into the hall.

He didn't stop there. Instead, he pulled her into the foyer where mistletoe hung from the archway. She looked beautiful today in a crimson dress that flowed over her once again slender figure. ''Your father told me he was wrong about me.''

''Good. It's about time.'' Jenna's smile was wide and knowing. ''Is that why you brought me out here? To tell me that?''

When he gazed down on her, an expansive love filled his whole being. ''No. I brought you out here because I suddenly had the urge to kiss you silly.''

''Kiss me silly or kiss me well?'' she asked coyly.

''You decide,'' he whispered as he bent his head, covered her lips with his and sent up a grateful prayer for Jenna and everything she'd brought him.

After he ended the kiss, he could see the same dazed look in Jenna's eyes that he knew was in his. Their passion for each other hadn't diminished one iota. In fact, it grew steadily each day, along with their love.

''You *are* a good kisser,'' she remarked teasingly. ''You make me forget we have guests for dinner.''

Blake reached into his pocket and brought out a small wrapped box. ''I was going to give this to you later when we exchange gifts, but I can't wait to see you wearing it.''

Jenna took the box and smiled up at him while she unwrapped it. He took the paper and bow from her and laid it on the foyer table as she opened the velvet box. ''Oh, Blake. It's beautiful!''

Inside lay a solid gold Florentine heart, engraved with Blake's name and Jenna's. From the point of the large heart dangled a smaller heart etched with a capital *E* for Elizabeth.

He could see Jenna's eyes grow moist as she took the necklace out of the box and turned her back to Blake. Taking advantage of the intimate moment, he placed a kiss on her neck, let his lips linger, then fastened the gold chain.

When she turned toward him again, her dark eyes were velvet with her love. "Merry Christmas, Blake."

Taking her into his arms once more, he kissed her, wishing her the very merriest and blessed of Christmases, promising her love that would last a lifetime and longer.

*   *   *   *   *

*Watch for Karen Rose Smith's next book
from Silhouette Romance,*

THE MOST ELIGIBLE DOCTOR,

coming in October 2003.

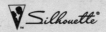

SPECIAL EDITION™

and

bestselling author

LAURIE PAIGE

introduce a new series about seven cousins—
bound by blood, honor and tradition—who bring
a whole new meaning to "family reunion"!

This time, the Daltons are the good guys....

"Laurie Paige doesn't miss..."
—*New York Times* bestselling author
Catherine Coulter

"It is always a joy to savor the consistent
excellence of this outstanding author."
—*Romantic Times*

Available at your favorite retail outlet.

Where love comes alive™

Visit Silhouette at www.eHarlequin.com

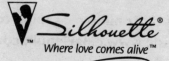

If you enjoyed what you just read,
then we've got an offer you can't resist!

Take 2 bestselling
love stories FREE!
Plus get a FREE surprise gift!

Clip this page and mail it to Silhouette Reader Service™

IN U.S.A.
3010 Walden Ave.
P.O. Box 1867
Buffalo, N.Y. 14240-1867

IN CANADA
P.O. Box 609
Fort Erie, Ontario
L2A 5X3

YES! Please send me 2 free Silhouette Special Edition® novels and my free surprise gift. After receiving them, if I don't wish to receive anymore, I can return the shipping statement marked cancel. If I don't cancel, I will receive 6 brand-new novels every month, before they're available in stores! In the U.S.A., bill me at the bargain price of $3.99 plus 25¢ shipping and handling per book and applicable sales tax, if any*. In Canada, bill me at the bargain price of $4.74 plus 25¢ shipping and handling per book and applicable taxes**. That's the complete price and a savings of at least 10% off the cover prices—what a great deal! I understand that accepting the 2 free books and gift places me under no obligation ever to buy any books. I can always return a shipment and cancel at any time. Even if I never buy another book from Silhouette, the 2 free books and gift are mine to keep forever.

235 SDN DNUR
335 SDN DNUS

Name	(PLEASE PRINT)	
Address	Apt.#	
City	State/Prov.	Zip/Postal Code

* Terms and prices subject to change without notice. Sales tax applicable in N.Y.
** Canadian residents will be charged applicable provincial taxes and GST.
All orders subject to approval. Offer limited to one per household and not valid to current Silhouette Special Edition® subscribers.
® are registered trademarks of Harlequin Books S.A., used under license.

SPED02   ©1998 Harlequin Enterprises Limited

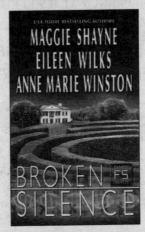

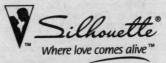

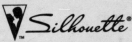

COMING NEXT MONTH